SCARY

FROM 1313 WICKED WAY

STORIES

Written by
CRAIG STRICKLAND

Lowell House
Juvenile
Los Angeles

CONTEMPORARY BOOKS
Chicago

Cover illustration: James McConnell

ISBN: 1-56565-484-6

Library of Congress Catalog Card Number: 96-2984

Publisher: Jack Artenstein
General Manager, Juvenile Division: Elizabeth Amos
Director of Publishing Services: Rena Copperman
Editor in Chief of Fiction, Juvenile Division: Barbara Schoichet
Managing Editor, Juvenile Division: Lindsey Hay
Art Director: Lisa-Theresa Lenthall
Cover and Interior Designer: Cheryl Carrington

Lowell House books can be purchased at special discounts
when ordered in bulk for premiums and special sales.
Contact Department JH at the following address:

Lowell House Juvenile
2029 Century Park East, Suite 3290
Los Angeles, CA 90067

Manufactured in the United States of America

10 9 8 7 6 5 4 3 2 1

CONTENTS

For Daniel and Sarah

—C.S.

The wagon pulled up over a little hill, and there it was, in a clearing. Instantly, the horses came to a dead halt, snorting, throwing their heads back, and rearing.

"Ladies, here is our new home," Samantha's father said proudly. "Built entirely by prison labor."

Samantha stared at the two-story mansion, its sparkling, multipaned windows like so many eyes looking at her. A shiver traced itself along her spine. It was the same feeling she'd had at her grandfather's funeral a year ago, when she'd looked into the coffin at his powdered dead face. Somehow, there was something "dead" about this house, too.

The house was Victorian, its front constructed of gray stone and wood. The dark brown roof was peaked at four places, and snarling gargoyles perched high on the rain gutters. Black shingles hung over the windows like brooding brows. And the whole place had a shadowy feeling to it which even the bright flowers bordering the tidy brick walk could not soften.

Samantha groaned quietly. *This* was the home of her father's dreams? Maybe it would have looked different—more like other people's dreams—if her father, Jack Jardine, wasn't the State Prison Warden. Yes, the house that Jack Jardine had built must have reminded him of the penitentiary he ruled over so fiercely, the penitentiary just five miles down the road. But how, Samantha wondered, could her father see this house at 1313 Wicket Way as his beautiful dream house? As far as she was concerned it looked nightmarish enough that the address could have been changed to 1313 *Wicked* Way.

"We'll have to hike our things in from here," her father said cheerfully, jumping from the wagon.

"Why not take the wagon closer, dear?" her mother asked, looking out from under a huge sunbonnet.

"Horses won't go any closer," he explained.

Sure enough, the horses were dancing excitedly in place, their eyes rolling back in their heads clear to the whites. "The same thing happens every time I've been to this place," the large, overbearing man continued. "Dumb animals—must be snake holes or something around here."

Climbing down from her seat, Samantha looked around among the oaks and tiny pines, trying to find what had spooked the horses. But there were no snake holes. The only thing she could see in the whole clearing was that horrible house her father loved so much, rising like a cold black tower in the forest.

Once inside, Samantha still felt ill at ease, even though Uncle Jacob, who had helped her father in drawing up the plans for the house, had come ahead and positioned all of their old furniture.

She walked through the high entry hall that was all carved in dark wood, examining the familiar tables and chairs in the dining room, the plush sofa in the living room, and the family portraits lining the hallway. On either side of the sweeping staircase were her father's latest acquisitions—two full suits of armor, both of which looked like they were guarding the upstairs. She paused to stare into the black eye holes, imagining that someone inside was staring back.

"Your mother and I have bedrooms on the top floor," her father said. Then he led her to a door next to the dining area and opened it. "I had to have your room put down here on the first floor because the men couldn't carry your piano up the stairs. I hope that's all right, Sam." He grinned. "At least you'll have lots of privacy, hmmm?"

"Yes, Father," Samantha said, entering the small room done up all in white, from the whitewashed wood on the walls to the billowing canopy over the bed. In the large corner stood her piano. She sighed with relief. It was like seeing an old friend "Thank you, Father," she said, turning to smile at him.

Her father smiled back, his thick bushy eyebrows raising with amusement. "Look around." he said. "Your mother will call you when dinner is ready."

After her father left, Samantha stared out of her window at the front walk leading into the woods. For some reason the sight made her feel gloomy. She sat at her piano to cheer herself up, but couldn't bring herself to play. Finally she stood and wandered about the house.

Upstairs, parts of the corridor were so dark Samantha could hardly see. She peeked in the doorways of the three large bedrooms, but the air inside was so cold that she felt extremely uncomfortable going into them and quickly stepped out. Finally she returned to her room, feeling more upset than before.

Why did this house make her feel so uneasy? There seemed to be something threatening about it, but Samantha couldn't figure out what it was. Her head swimming with fears her father would call childish, Samantha quickly erased them. "I'm just being silly," she scolded herself as she sat on her bed, her feet curled up under her, just in case something was underneath it that might make a grab for her. Across the room were the beautifully carved doors of a huge wardrobe closet. *Could a monster be inside there?* her fears began again.

Suddenly, her door swung open. Samantha jumped nearly a foot. "Dinnertime, Sam," said her mother cheerfully. And then she saw her daughter's white face. "What's the matter, dear?"

Samantha tried to smile, but failed. "I guess I just don't like this house, Mother."

"Now you listen to me, Samantha," her mother said sternly. "There's not a thing wrong with this house. It's the largest, most beautiful house for miles around."

"That's just because Father used convicts for free labor," Samantha mumbled. She'd never thought it had been very fair, and from the little bits of conversation she'd heard between her father and her Uncle Jacob, she gathered that her father had been rather cruel to the prisoners during the construction.

"Young lady, your father is very proud of this house. Don't you ever let him hear you say anything against it."

Samantha supposed her mother was right. Feeling drearier than ever, she went over to her window to look at the beautiful flowers that lined the brick walkway. But when she gazed out, all she could do was gasp. The pansies, the marigolds—all the flowers that she had noticed just a few hours before, were all dead!

"How odd," she murmured, staring at the drooping dead flowers. They weren't just wilted—each one had completely shriveled and turned the color of coal. Their blooms, like crumpled black bits of ash, lay lifeless on the ground.

That night, Samantha could not imagine how she would sleep in this creepy place. She lit a tall candle and placed it near her bed, hoping it would last until she could fall asleep. The flickering light created moving shadows that made her shudder, but anything was better than total darkness. She lay, tossing and turning, until finally she fell into a restless half-sleep.

The first sounds came at midnight. They were the faint tinkling sounds of metal on metal. Trying to decipher what the sounds were, Samantha finally decided they were chains. Terrified, she looked around the room. The candle had burned quite low, and in the dim light, all she could see was part of the floor.

A few minutes later, the candle, now only a stub of wax, burned out. Samantha held the pillow to her tightly pounding heart. And listened.

The rattling continued. It didn't seem to be in the room, but *under* the room, floating up from the floorboards below. And now there was another, deeper sound, a gurgling sound, also coming from beneath the floor. It began low and hollow, rising slowly in pitch, like the sound of a huge glass filling with water.

Samantha burrowed under her sheets as the chains rattled and the water noise rose, higher and higher. She moaned, unable to take it any longer. And just as the noise reached its highest pitch, everything abruptly stopped, leaving only the sound of the wind howling through the pines in the nearby forest.

Still trembling, Samantha yearned to run to her parents. But not only was she afraid she would be scolded for letting childish fears get the better of her, she was also too afraid to even set foot out of her bed. And so, for the rest of the night, Samantha lay there, her fingers digging into her pillow, waiting for the sounds to return.

At breakfast the next morning, Samantha poked at her toast, barely able to keep her eyes open, and unable to say anything. In fact, she had always found it hard to talk with her parents. They were the kind of people who seemed to have all kinds of secrets.

Finally, she could take it no more. She looked up at them. "Did either of you hear anything last night?"

"I don't recall hearing anything," her mother said. She turned to Samantha's father. "Did you, dear?"

Samantha's father shook his head. "What exactly did you hear, Sam?" he asked.

"Well, maybe I was imagining things . . ." Samantha began hesitantly, "but I thought I heard some chains rattling below my room." She paused. "And there was some kind of watery sound, too."

Samantha saw a look pass between her parents. Then her mother's face grew pale as chalk. She excused herself, rose from the table, and walked quickly from the room. Her father, too, stood up. "I've got to get to the prison," he said. "I'm sorry, but I haven't got time for such nonsense."

But her mother's reaction had frightened Samantha. "Father," she persisted, "what do you think I heard?"

"Nothing, dear," he said, his voice firm. "As you said, it was simply your imagination playing tricks on you."

Her father gave her a wide smile, but to Sam it looked false. It wasn't his usual smile, the one that put a twinkle in his eye. Now she could see something unusual in his eyes, something she had never seen there before. It was something like fear.

Later that morning, Samantha sat down at her piano as she did every day. But today she didn't feel like playing, and her fingers rested unmoving on the keys. She gazed out the window at the gardener, who planted fresh flowers along the walk. *Would they die, too?* she wondered. And what about the sounds she'd heard last night? They seemed to have come from the very earth below her room. That is, if there was earth below her room.

Suddenly the answer came to her. "This house has a basement!" she exclaimed to no one. "That's where the sounds are coming from!" Practically leaping off the piano bench, Samantha grabbed a candle from its holder on the wall and hurried down the hallway.

She circled slowly around the base of the stairs, looking carefully for some kind of entryway, and sure enough, there was a door, cut into one wall. For a moment, she hesitated. *What will I find down there?* she thought. Then, realizing there was only one way to find out, she opened the door, grimacing as it squeaked like a yowling cat.

Taking a deep breath and gripping the candle so tightly her fingers ached, Samantha crept down the dark steps into a small, empty room. There, she held the flame next to the brick walls, carefully examining their gleaming surface, wet with some kind of moisture.

Next she held the candle close to the brick floor. "These scratches look almost like words," she murmured. She looked closer, squinting in the dim light. *Something had* been written there, carved into the hard surface with a sharp instrument. And then her heart froze as she read the startling message: A CURSE ON THIS HOUSE!

"One of the prisoners must have cut this message into the floor!" Samantha cried. "But why?"

Suddenly the candlelight picked up something shiny. Samantha looked down and saw three chains, each with an attached leg iron, set into the stone floor. *No!* she thought. *These chains couldn't be the ones I heard last night. Chains don't rattle by themselves!*

But the thought set her to trembling so much that Samantha accidentally dropped her candle. Instantly, the flame extinguished. Plunged into darkness, she frantically bent down and felt for the candle, but her hand fell on one of the chains instead. With a shriek, she pulled her hand away. The chains were so cold, it felt like they had been encased in ice for thousands of years. Not daring to reach for the candle again, Samantha frantically began to feel her way up the stairs in total blackness.

Someone was waiting for her at the top.

"*Ahhhh!*" she screamed, then gasped with relief when she saw who it was.

"My, you're jumpy lately!" her mother exclaimed, shaking her head and smiling. "What on earth were you doing down there in the first place?"

"I—I was just looking around," Samantha stammered, her heart still racing. "I think something happened in this basement, Mother. Something terrible!" She rubbed her hands together because they were still numb from the cold chain.

"Listen, Samantha, I don't want you going down there again," her mother said sternly. "There could be rats."

"Tell me everything, Mother!" Samantha cried. "Tell me everything you know about this awful house!"

But her mother turned away. "All I know is that the basement isn't safe . . . and I want you staying out of there."

And with that she walked swiftly down the narrow hallway, her wide hoop dress almost touching each wall.

As she began to make her way to her room, Samantha saw her father out by the entry. He was scowling and obviously in no mood to talk with her either.

As he looked out the front door, shaking his head at something, he glanced at Samantha, and jabbed a finger at the walkway in front of the house.

"Look at that," he muttered. "I guess we have to find *another* new gardener. All the flowers are dead again."

That night Samantha filled her room with candles. Then she lay wrapped in the sheets, convinced she'd be awake all night, staring at the underside of her canopy and shaking in fear. But as the hours went by, her eyelids drooped. The combination of having a near sleepless night the day before and moving in to a new home had exhausted her, and finally she drifted off to a night filled with odd dreams. She was filling huge glasses of water, over and over again, and heavy chains rattled from her wrists.

The next day Samantha's Uncle Jacob came by early in the morning. He had always been kind to Samantha, and she trusted him. Since he had been in charge of overseeing the construction of the house, Samantha felt that her uncle might be the one person who could clear up a few things.

"Why are there chains in the basement?" she asked, as soon as they were alone in the yard.

"So, you've been poking around the place," he said, ruffling her hair. He paused for a moment and the smile that had been on his face disappeared. "Your father and I used those chains to secure the prisoners at night."

Samantha thought about telling her uncle about how the chains seemed to rattle at night, but was afraid he'd dismiss it all as her imagination just as her father had done. She decided to take a different approach. "Did any of the prisoners who worked on the house ever die, Uncle Jacob?" she asked. "You know, while they were working?"

He looked at her strangely. "Of course not. A few suffered injuries while on the job, but no one died." A grin crept onto his face. "Of course, I don't know for sure about the landscapers."

Samantha was confused. "What do you mean?"

"Well, there were three other men who were brought from the prison to pour the cement for the little fishpond to the side of the house. They were also supposed to plant all the trees, lay out the lawn, and put in the flowers. Your father was in charge of them." Her uncle chuckled, then gazed at the blackened plants around him. "Obviously they weren't very talented gardeners. From the looks of this yard, it appears that prison laborers make better house builders than they do landscapers, wouldn't you say?"

Suddenly a low rumble of thunder rippled across the skies. "Let's go inside," Uncle Jacob said. "It looks like its going to rain and that's enough talk about prisoners."

Sure enough, by late morning the clouds had massed into a solid black fist that threatened to open at any moment and throw down a hard rain. But no matter how it poured, the rain couldn't be as strong as it reportedly had been the week before when the house at 1313 Wicket Way was being finished. That week it had rained buckets every day, causing floods all over the countryside.

Looking at the dark sky, Samantha decided to spend as much time outdoors as possible before the storm hit. First she strolled past her father's fishpond, admiring the lily pads and darting shapes beneath the water's surface. Then she turned to explore the woods.

At first thinking it dark and foreboding, Samantha soon realized that the forest was really very pretty once she went into it a little deeper. The trees were lush and green, and the ground was sprinkled with wildflowers. But whenever she drew closer to the house, the trees became smaller and unhealthy looking. Nothing at all seemed to be able to grow near the place. In fact, the few trees which stood next to the structure itself were dead and bleached white, looking almost like dried bones.

Curious, Samantha spent the rest of the afternoon circling the property, wondering if she could find *anything* that was alive and growing. Then, just before suppertime, she noticed an odd collection of tumble-weeds clumped together as if covering something. When she moved the tumbleweeds aside, she found three long mounds of dirt. "Graves!" she gasped, staggering backward. "So people *did* die here. I knew it!"

Suddenly a tremendous peal of thunder boomed from the sky, and the clouds let go. Samantha ran back through the black, dead yard in front of the house, but before she got there she was soaked right through her clothes.

She burst into the dining room, her dress dripping all over the floor.

"Where have you been?" her father asked, rising from the table, a frown of concern on his face.

"I found three graves!" Samantha cried. "And I think three prisoners who worked on our house are buried—!"

"That's none of your concern!" her mother snapped. She rose from the table, ready to walk away, as usual.

12

But this time, Samantha wouldn't let her. "Wait!" she called after her, catching her mother by the arm. "We have to leave here! There's a curse on this house. I saw it written in the—"

"Go to your room!" her father barked. "I will not tolerate another word of this nonsense!" He stood and took a step toward her, his eyes blazing. But once again, Samantha saw more fear than anger.

She ran around the corner to her bedroom and slammed the door behind her. Then she lit all of her candles and placed them everywhere she could, lighting every inch of the room. Filled with frustration, she threw herself on the bed and sobbed as the rain poured down outside her window.

But all of a sudden, Samantha heard her parents arguing in the next room.

"If only you didn't *chain* them there," her mother was saying in a hushed tone.

"It's not like they were human beings!" her father yelled back. "They were prisoners. They didn't deserve any better!"

A thunderclap crashed outside so close to the house that it made the windowpanes rattle. Straining to hear over the violent downpour, Samantha heard only snatches of words here and there. Then her parents' voices grew distant as they headed upstairs. She did hear one thing, however, loud and clear from her father: "How was I to know they would drown?" he bellowed. "Tell me that!"

A chill, like an ice cold wind, passed through Samantha as she pictured the room below her filling with water and drowning the three men, each chained to the wall like a forgotten animal. But obviously the three drowned convicts *didn't* forget. For once again Samantha heard the sound of chains rattling, chains she knew held the spirits of three very angry men. *How long can chains hold a spirit?* she asked herself. *How long until they break free and seek their revenge?*

Laying in bed, her eyes wide, Samantha suddenly got her answer. As the rain streamed down the window and giant bolts of lightning crashed from the sky, she realized what was happening. The horrible storm that had killed the convicts was repeating itself. Once again the basement was flooding. And once again the convicts were straining against their chains.

But this time, filled with ghostly power, filled with a terrible revenge, the convicts were breaking free, tearing their shackles from the basement walls and now—as Samantha already heard—they were thumping and clanging upstairs.

"Samantha?" she heard her father call. "Is that you on the stairs?"

"It's not me, Father!" Samantha screamed. "It's—"

But her warning was too late. Suddenly the house was alive with the shrieks of her parents. First her father's cries stopped, then her mother's, then a deathly silence fell throughout the house.

Samantha whimpered as the sound of chains echoed on the stairs—this time slowly making their way down—*thump clang, thump clang,* one step at a time. Huddling in the corner, she waited . . . as they came for her.

DEATH SONG – 1868

An old grand piano stood in the gloom, its keys yellow like rotten teeth. Inside the piano bench, nothing but moth-eaten scraps remained of the sheet music. In fact, a visitor might find it hard to believe that the piano had ever been played. For the entire room it stood in was quiet as death.

Outside, the happy voices of a family came from the woods. Four people on three horses rode into view—a mother, a father, and their two sons. Tying the animals to a tree, the family dismounted and stood staring at the house, their joyous conversations stunned into silence by the ominous sight.

As if in reaction to newcomers, something inside the piano room stirred. It was the piano's bench, which suddenly squeaked as if settling under the weight of a pianist. Next the key-cover flicked back with a snap. And finally, the tiny hammers inside the instrument began to strike at the old steel strings. The song that filled the room was as light as spring, at first, but within seconds it deepened, sounding frantic and frightening, dark like a gathering storm.

"Isn't that piano music?" Peter, the eldest son, asked. But as he listened, the notes seemed to fade away.

"Yes," his mother answered. "I think it was."

His father and six-year-old brother, John, only shrugged.

"Must have been the wind," Peter offered. Still, he couldn't help staring at the strange deserted house before him. He couldn't believe the place was only seventy years old. It looked *centuries* older than that.

The entire two stories seemed to be rotting. Paint hung off in huge patches like peeling dead skin. Loose shingles lay scattered on the roof. Oddly, none of the many windowpanes were broken. Most, however, were cracked, and the design the cracks formed looked like the lines of a huge spider web across the face of the building. Above everything, high on the roof, several gargoyles, each wearing a thick cloak of mold, peered at them with unseeing eyes.

Peter's mother shook her head. "Some inheritance."

John hopped excitedly next to Peter, sending up clouds of dust. The ground was cracked and black and nothing grew from it, not even weeds. "It looks like a haunted house!" he shrieked happily. "Maybe we'll find a ghost!"

Their father chuckled. "Lots of folks have thought this place was haunted, but I don't believe it." He stroked his long sideburns thoughtfully. "Still, it is a gloomy-looking place, isn't it, boys?"

Twelve-year-old Peter shuddered. He'd heard the story about the old mansion many times. Apparently, his father's great-aunt and uncle were killed here many years ago. They were found beheaded upstairs in their beds. The authorities were sure their daughter, Samantha, was killed, too, although they never found her body.

Through the years, the family had continually passed off the horrible incident, saying that the parents and daughter were killed by evil spirits. Peter believed it was true. But not his father. He was a practical man who didn't believe in anything concerning the supernatural. He believed his great-aunt and uncle, along with their little girl, were killed by some murderous drifter.

"Mother?" Peter tugged gently on her sleeve. "Do you believe evil spirits killed Father's relatives?"

His mother's eyes never left the strangely cracked windows of the old mansion. "I don't know, Peter," she said. "All the same, I can see why no one in the family was ever able to live here for more than a few days."

"Well, we're not going to live here, either," Peter's father reminded them. "We're only here to look around our property, to see if there's anything valuable, and to decide if it's worth fixing up to sell." He took a step toward the crumbling brick walk that led to the huge wooden front door. "We've still got a few hours of daylight left. There's bound to be some interesting things inside. I even remember Great Grandfather Jacob telling me about some secret passages. So, who's going to join me?"

"Me, me!" John yelled. "I'm coming with you, Papa!"

"I'll come, too," their mother said hesitantly.

Peter, at the mere mention of secret passages, had already darted ahead of his father and was leading the way to the front door.

It took the whole family pushing on it, but finally the heavy old door squeaked open in a puff of dust. In the entryway, Peter's father lit a candle for each person except John, then handed them out.

Holding his candle for both himself and his little brother, Peter could make out two staircases heading into the darkness above. He started to head for them with John on his heels.

"Boys, stay on this floor until we check out those stairs," their father warned. Then he and their mother went into a formal dining room.

"And keep within earshot!" their mother called. "I don't want you wandering off in this eerie old place."

The boys looked at each other, then at the hallway. Spiderwebs hung everywhere. "Where do you s'pose the secret passages are?" John asked, his eyes eager.

Peter glanced around them. "We might as well start looking in this hall. There might be something behind these paintings." He carefully held his candle up to the nearest picture, an old oil painting of a girl with a big ribbon in her sandy brown hair. She was posing before a piano. Her mouth was set in a deadly serious straight line. All at once it came to Peter who it was.

"Samantha," he muttered, as if she were actually there instead of just in the picture.

John was quiet for several seconds. He stared at the painting fearfully, then took a step closer to his big brother. "Do you think *her* head was cut off, too?"

Peter only looked at his little brother. "How do you know about that?"

John shrugged. "I heard Mama and Papa talking."

Peter looked at his brother sternly, then cracked a smile. "Well, you shouldn't be eavesdropping," he said, remembering that he had heard the story the same way.

"Do you think we might find her body somewhere?" John persisted.

"It's possible. Of course, she'd probably just be bones by now," Peter answered. Then he turned away from the painting. It was better not to get John's imagination going about things like dead bodies. "Anyway, don't worry about that. We want to find a secret passage, right? Come on. Let's try knocking on the wall panels to see if any sound hollow."

For the next few minutes, the two boys circled the walls, examining and rapping lightly on them. Finally, John's voice rang out, "Peter! I found one!"

Peter raced over to where his brother crouched at a low panel just under the stairwell on the left. "Listen!" John said excitedly. He rapped at the wood, and a hollow echo sounded back.

"Good job," Peter said, grinning. He pushed on the panel and pressed at various places. Then the entire square swung out like a little door.

"Wow!" John gasped. "Wait'll Papa sees this!"

The boys leaned into the opening. The passageway seemed to go on and on. Peter's attention was drawn to a long cluster of white objects on the floor inside. He moved closer, squinting and holding out his candle. Startled, Peter backed out. The flickering light had lit up a trail of bones that led right down the passage. Apparently, John had seen the bones, too, for now he stood wide-eyed and speechless.

"I know what you're thinking," Peter said, trying to keep his voice calm. "But those bones are tiny. They're probably not human bones. They must be from—"

Suddenly, the house was filled with the notes of a piano. Peter's trembling fingers dug into the wax of his candle. It was the same music he had heard when they were standing outside the house. Once again, the melody started gently, then rose in a menacing way.

The boys hurried down the hall, and as the music abruptly halted, their parents came rushing out of the dining room. "Was that you two?" their mother asked.

"We were over there," Peter said, pointing back down the hallway. "In fact, we thought it was you."

"I think it came from that front room," their father said. "Has anyone been in there yet?"

They all shook their heads. Then all four of them cautiously entered through the open doorway of the room just off the dining area. The remains of an ancient canopy bed stood in the center of the room, the material torn and drooping in rotted ribbons. Next to the bed stood a frilly dresser with a broken leg that caused it to tilt against the wall. Crouching like some huge animal in the corner was a gorgeous, but very old, piano.

Peter stepped back as though he'd seen a rattlesnake. "I bet this was Samantha's room," he whispered.

"Yes," their father agreed. "And I bet this is a player piano. That's what we must have heard."

"You mean like the kind that plays music using a piano roll?" Peter asked doubtfully.

His father nodded, scratching his chin. "And it was probably a rat or a squirrel that ran over the pedals, causing the piano to start playing." He smiled, as he walked over to the beautiful instrument and patted it on its heavy wooden top. He looked back at his wife, who still stood uncertainly in the doorway. "Come on, dear," he said to her. "Help me get this thing open. We can be sure if we look inside."

"Father, no!" Peter yelled out. "Get away from it!"

The piano was beginning to terrify him. What if Samantha's killer had hidden her body *inside* her own piano? Wouldn't that be reason enough for her to haunt it?

Peter's father set his candleholder on the piano and crossed his arms sternly. "Is this about ghosts again?"

Peter looked at his shoes.

"When strange things happen, there's always a logical explanation," his father said in a calm tone. And with that he flipped open the keyboard cover for a second. The row of ivory surfaces looked like a wide, ugly smile. "This *has* to be a player piano. All I want to do is check."

Sighing, Peter's mother entered the room and walked briskly over to the piano. "Well, all right, then, I'll help. If only to dismiss this nonsense about ghosts."

First they batted away the cobwebs that practically covered the top of the old instrument. Then together, Peter's parents struggled with the lid. Slowly, it began to creak open, causing flakes of paint to scatter onto the floor.

John stood excitedly on his tiptoes, trying to peek inside, as his parents continued to work off the aged cover. But Peter, who stood back, felt sick. If his hunch was right, it would be just like opening a coffin. He thought of the serious-faced girl in the picture. Would she be wrapped up like the mummies he'd seen at the museum? Or would her skeleton be scrunched up in a little corner of the piano she'd loved so much?

Finally, the lid was raised, and Peter's father propped it open with the wide support stick he found inside. Then, holding their candles down into the piano, both his parents peered over the edge into the scary-looking instrument.

Suddenly, Peter had a clear picture of what was going to happen. That heavy lid was going to fall, and his parents' heads were going to be chopped off, just like his father's great-uncle and aunt. "Mother! Father!" Peter shouted. "Get away!"

Startled, his parents jerked their heads back out of the piano, and to his horror, Peter saw the supporting stick crack, then splinter in two. An instant later, the lid crashed down with a heavy thud, followed by an eerie echo of jangled piano notes that resounded for several minutes afterward.

Slumping against the side of the terrible instrument, his body twitching, Peter's father's face contorted in pain. "Help me," he whispered as he pointed to his right arm, still trapped inside the piano up to the shoulder.

Peter jumped forward to help while his mother struggled with the lid. John, who had burst out crying, stood off to the side, trembling.

Finally, using his other hand for support, Peter's father eased his arm out. "It's broken," he said weakly.

"Oh, sweetheart!" Peter's mother cried, kneeling next to her husband. "We've got to get you to a doctor."

While Peter held his candle to give her light, his mother worked fast. First she peeled back her husband's bloody shirt to expose the grotesquely crooked arm.

Then, quickly fashioning a splint from a piece of the very same wood that had once held up the lid, she set it in place with some fabric torn from the canopy bed.

"Now, boys, listen to me carefully," she said. "I've got to help your father get to a town that has a doctor. Peter, I want you to stay here and watch after your brother."

Peter stared at her, amazed. He shook his head hard. "Mother, you can't leave us here alone! Didn't you see what just happened with that piano?"

"Peter, when you yelled at us, your father must have bumped into the piano lid!" his mother said angrily, then quickly softened her tone. "Now, I know you didn't do it on purpose, but those are the facts!"

John started blubbering again. Speechless, Peter could only shake his head. They thought *he* had caused the accident! Apparently, no one else had seen the supporting stick splinter all by itself.

"Anyway, John's not old enough to ride with anyone else but your father," his mother went on. "So, I'm going to count on you, Peter, to be the responsible one here." She paused for a moment as if thinking. "There's food and blankets in the saddlebags. With a little luck, we should be back before dark. If not, you can sleep in here. It's the only bedroom on this floor, and I still don't want you going upstairs." She pointed at the sagging canopy bed. "That bed is a little musty, but it looks fine."

"But, Mother," Peter insisted. "This house isn't safe."

"Not another *word*," she said, growing annoyed. "This is an emergency."

"I'm afraid your mother's right," Peter's father said through gritted teeth. "Do as she says."

Within minutes, Peter's mother had bundled up his father, and they were heading out the door. For a moment, his father turned and smiled weakly at Peter before hobbling down the brick walkway. "I *still* think it's a player piano," he called back, joking.

As he watched his parents leave, Peter held John's hand tightly, and together they stood at the front door until the sounds of hoofbeats faded in the distance.

"Poor Papa," John muttered once they were alone. He shuddered. "I don't like it here, Peter."

"Me, neither," Peter answered, planting a false smile on his face. Now, without their parents here, it would be a disaster to scare his little brother by sharing his own fears. "Hey, you brought your ball in the saddlebag, right? Want to throw it around outside for a couple of minutes?"

John nodded eagerly, and for the next hour they tossed about the six-year-old's favorite ball, the one with the face of a colorful smiling clown drawn on its surface. As the boys played, the mansion's shadow grew steadily longer and longer, spreading like a black blanket over the lifeless ground. At last the sun crawled over the hill, setting behind the house. All light bled away, making the old mansion appear bigger and darker than ever against the black sky.

"Hey!" John shouted, looking along the side of the house after one of Peter's throws went wild. "I can't see where the ball went!"

Peter went over to help him, but the boys gave up in defeat after several minutes. "It's too dark. Let's go inside," Peter said, even though the thought of entering the foreboding house churned his stomach. "We'll look for your ball tomorrow." He cast a final glance at the woods, hoping to see their parents come riding back. But all he saw was the one remaining horse, standing among a bunch of twisted pines reaching toward the evening sky.

Peter lit a candle, and they walked back inside the mansion. The hall seemed immense in the dark, and the place felt much colder than during the daytime. All Peter could think about was running down the hall to shut the panel of the secret passage. He could picture it, hanging open the way they'd left it, the strange little bones still scattered along its floor.

Putting it out of his mind so as not to scare John, he quickly led his brother to the piano room and shut the door behind them.

"I *really* don't like this room," John whined.

"Well, we might end up sleeping here, so get used to it," Peter said firmly. He paused for a moment and tried to put a kinder tone in his voice. "Are you hungry?"

John shook his head, staring about the room.

"Me, neither," Peter said. "I don't think our candles will last much longer. Guess we'd better try to get some sleep." He walked toward the bed, trying to avoid looking at the corner where the piano seemed to lurk in the shadows. "John, listen," he said suddenly. "Let's just stay in our clothes, all right? That way when Mother and Father come for us, we can get right out of here."

John agreed readily and began to help his brother turn down the bed. The linen on the old bed was dusty and threadbare, but the mattress was still intact. They laid their blankets on the rotted bedclothes and, leaving a candle flickering at the bedside, the two brothers climbed in. Staring at the shadows on the walls cast by the dying candle, both boys tossed and turned for nearly an hour. Then, with the wind whispering in the forest, they finally drifted off into an uneasy sleep.

At midnight, something stirred in the old room. As the boys slept, a shadow passed over the canopy bed. Then the piano bench squeaked.

Peter's eyes flew open. Someone—or some*thing*—was sitting at the piano! His heart racing, Peter peered at the figure, illuminated by the moonlight that streamed in through the tattered lace curtains.

"Samantha?" Peter gasped, seeing that the figure was a girl, her hands raised over the piano keys, ready to play.

The girl's hands fell to her lap. Slowly, she turned, and Peter could see that she wasn't a ghost, or a girl at all. Instead, he found himself staring at an old, wrinkled woman, bent over in the moonlight. Her face, framed by her flowing white hair, was thin and bony, reminding Peter of a skull. And her eyes, peering out of sunken eye sockets, glittered with what he thought might be insanity.

"How did you know my name?" the tiny old woman croaked. It was like hearing a child speaking with the cracked voice of someone much older.

Peter swallowed. "I—I thought you were . . ."

Samantha smiled, revealing crooked, stained teeth. "I've lived here in this house all my life," she said. "Who are you? I haven't seen another child in years."

"Another child?" Peter whispered.

"Why, yes," the old woman said matter-of-factly. "I'm only twelve, you know." She stood and curtsied, then pointed to a panel just like the one they had found in the hall. Somehow, without Peter's noticing it, the panel had opened on the wall to one side of the piano. "I noticed you found one of my secret passages. Would you like to see others? I've lived in them for years." She leaned forward as if confiding something. "Lots of rats in there, you know. If you're hungry, I could catch you one." She rubbed her vein-covered hands together in a greedy gesture.

Peter thought of all the little white bones they'd seen in the passage in the hall. *Rat bones!* he thought, his stomach churning. *John and I found the place where Samantha threw her leftovers!*

Suddenly, John awoke "What's going on?" he asked, his eyes wide with fright as he stared at the ancient woman.

"I don't know," Peter said quietly. "But it looks like there are no ghosts or haunted pianos in this house, after all." He pointed to the white-haired person before them, feeling pity now instead of fear. "Just one lonely little girl rattling around a mansion and scaring everybody."

Samantha cocked her head in an expression of surprise. "Oh, I'm not lonely. I've got my parents, and *lots* of other company here." She giggled like a child. "I've been trying to reach them with my piano ever since you came. You see, the song brings them." She turned back toward the piano. "Here, let me try to call them again."

John grabbed Peter's arm. "Don't let her do it, Peter!" he cried. But Samantha was already sitting at the bench, her fingers raised and coming down onto the keys.

Lightly at first, like a springtime melody, the music came forth, slowly turning more dramatic. Something was going to happen. Peter could feel it.

"We have to get out of here." But his brother only whimpered and clung to him, struck dumb with fear.

As he tried to pry John off him and untangle the two of them from the blankets, Peter heard footsteps coming from somewhere in the house followed by a whistling, hissing sound. Then, a second later, the door to the bedroom banged open, revealing two adult shapes. They were swaying slightly as if rocking to the music, and they looked perfectly normal . . . except they were nearly transparent and had no heads.

"Mother! Father!" Samantha cried. "I wanted you to meet my new friends!"

Samantha's parents stumbled toward her. With a shriek, Peter grabbed his sobbing brother. "Run!" he yelled. "Run for your life, John!"

Together the two boys scrambled around the ghosts and out the door, their hearts pounding. Once in the hall, they could hear a terrible moaning rising like a chant all through the house. Then chains began rattling from somewhere below.

Bursting out the front door, clutching John's hand, Peter ran down the brick walk. The piano music rang in his ears as he mounted the horse, pulled his brother up in front of him, and galloped off into the dark forest.

The eerie music continued to beat in Peter's brain as he rode away from the terrible house like a madman. And somewhere in the back of his mind he knew it would continue to do so for the rest of his life.

The pack of howling wolves was no more than a quarter mile behind them. Jimmy ran through the dark cold forest, his bedroll bouncing on his hip. Branches scratched his face, and with every step he took, Jimmy had to fight to keep from sinking into the thick powdery snow. His father trotted just ahead of him, and as he ran Jimmy tried to fit his feet into his father's larger tracks.

"That's a boy, Jimmy!" his father shouted over his shoulder between breaths, his words slightly slurred. "We'll beat 'em, don't worry. That shortcut has to be somewhere around here. We just . . ."

His words were drowned out by the howling wolves, howling that had gotten louder as the wolves drew closer.

It wasn't the first time Jimmy's father had gotten them lost in the forest on one of his little "shortcuts." It was hard enough trying to have a life with a father who wandered from town to town looking for work, but what made it worse was that often his father couldn't even *find* the next town. Jimmy knew the reason why—it was all because of his father's drinking. Even now, as they ran, Jimmy could see the bottle sticking out of the pocket of the man's tattered jacket. He steadied it with one hand as if it were the most important thing in the world to him.

As he ran behind his father, Jimmy couldn't help but wonder what the man might have been capable of if he could've just stopped drinking? He might have been able to hold down a steady job. He might have been able to have provided Jimmy with a proper home. And most of all, he might have made it possible for Jimmy's mother to live with them again.

"Come on, boy!" his father yelled encouragingly as the two began to scramble up a little hill.

Jimmy looked back over his shoulder. The wolves were now only a few hundred yards away. Their yellow eyes glowed in the moonlight. "Father!" he gasped. "Maybe we should climb a tree."

"No, we're gonna make it," his father insisted. "Look!"

There, down in the barren meadow, stood the black silhouette of a house. Something about the sharp, crooked line of the roof and the dull glint of its windows made Jimmy stop in his tracks, but then he glanced back and saw the pack of wolves right at his heels.

"Run for the house, boy!" his father yelled. *Run!*

The two dodged through the trees. His heart nearly pounding from his chest, Jimmy was sure they'd never make it, and then all of a sudden he realized that the howling coming from the wolves had grown more distant.

Stopping for a brief moment to glance over his shoulder, Jimmy couldn't believe his eyes. "Father! Look!"

For a moment father and son stood in awed silence, watching the wolves. The animals were pacing right at the edge of the barren meadow. It was as if they knew the ground had been poisoned.

"Wonder what spooked 'em," his father said, his eyes fixed on the wolves who seemed to be looking beyond the breathless humans at the dark house that lay ahead. Then, all at once, the entire pack tucked their tails between their legs and skulked back out of sight into the forest.

"Well, whatever it was sure saved us," Jimmy replied.

His father grinned. "Don't think I've ever had a closer call than that," he admitted, then turned and began walking slowly toward the rundown looking house. "Come on, boy. Let's go have a look at the place."

Angrily, Jimmy trudged behind his father. Neither of them would have had such a close call if his father would start acting like a father. He was just about to speak his mind, when suddenly his anger was replaced with a feeling of nervousness. It was as if he felt someone was watching them . . . someone unfriendly.

It's just the wolves, he told himself. *I'm still worried they'll come after us.* He glanced back several times, expecting to see the creatures bolt out of the trees and renew the chase, but they were gone. Then Jimmy looked ahead, and he knew immediately what was bothering him.

It was the house. The contrast between the bright snow and the mansion's stark outline made it seem the darkest thing Jimmy had ever seen—blacker than coal. Did his father feel it, too? For now the man had stopped and was staring hard at the towering cold structure. A trellis, covered with traces of ancient dead vines, climbed toward the upper windows. But no light shone through the panes, and no smoke curled from the chimney.

"Must be deserted," Jimmy's father decided as he neared the back porch. "There's no footprints—animal or human." He scratched thoughtfully at his beard-stubbled chin. "Well, let's find a way in, boy."

Jimmy's father went right up to the back door and rattled the knob, but the door didn't budge. "Ah, I knew it wouldn't be that easy," he grumbled. "Let's try the front, then we can see if there's any broken windows."

They began to walk off, when a high squeaking sound moaned into the night air. The pair turned around and stared. The back door had swung wide open. Jimmy felt his scalp tingle. No doubt about it—there was something very strange about this place.

"Well, I'll be . . ." his father muttered. "I must have loosened it when I twisted the knob."

Jimmy paused, staring at the house that seemed to wait for them like a spider awaiting its prey. *The place is haunted,* Jimmy thought fearfully. *That's why the wolves stopped chasing us once we got near the house.*

His father bounded up the porch steps, then turned to his son, still standing several feet away. "Come on, Jimmy. It'll be warmer inside," he said with a confident smile. "It's just an old house—nothing to be afraid of."

Jimmy watched as his father followed his "courageous" words by uncapping his bottle and downing a nervous swig of whiskey. Shaking his head at the hated bottle, Jimmy glanced up at the tar-black house before him. "I'm not afraid, Father," he said as cheerfully as he could muster. "Lead the way!"

His father eyed him suspiciously, then fumbled in his jacket pocket for the box of long matches he always carried. Unfortunately, the two had run out of candles several towns ago, so the matches would have to be their only source of light. He scratched one to life. Then father and son smiled bravely at each other, and stepped into the quiet darkness of the mansion in the woods.

Once inside, Jimmy and his father looked around in amazement. Nearly every wall was beautifully carved, and the remains of rich carpeting filled the hallways. *What a magnificent place to grow up,* Jimmy thought, remembering the cheap rented lodgings he'd been raised in.

"Well, we've certainly found ourselves a grand place," Jimmy's father declared. "I've never stayed in a two-story house before. How 'bout we sleep in one of the bedrooms upstairs tonight, boy?"

"Sounds great," Jimmy answered happily. Although the place still frightened him a bit, he hardly had to pretend anymore that he wasn't afraid. In fact, he was actually very glad to be out of the cold.

As the two made their way down the dark hallway toward a large, looming staircase, suddenly the tall match his father had lit burned out. Quickly Jimmy suppressed a gasp as the darkness engulfed him. Then, with his heart pounding so hard he could barely breathe, he heard his father shaking another match out of the box.

Hurry, Father! his mind screamed, as he peered around in the total blackness, certain that something in the shadows was pressing toward them. Finally his father scratched another match into life, and Jimmy's heart slowed back to normal.

"Ah, now there's a majestic staircase if I ever saw one!" his father declared. "Come, let's have a look upstairs."

The steps moaned beneath them as they climbed to the second floor, and on the way up, they marveled at the paintings that lined the walls. The picture on the ground level had been very disturbing to Jimmy. It was of a somber little girl, with eyes so sad and bewildered that she looked lost. Halfway up the staircase was a landscape painting, showing what appeared to be the forest in the nearby area, and on the next canvas was a man posed in an old-fashioned suit covered with ruffles, standing by a table of fruit. Both Jimmy and his father gasped at this painting—the man had no head!

"My goodness!" Jimmy's father cried, stepping back. The empty collar of the man in the painting was painted blood-red, and it looked as if he had been beheaded just seconds before the artist set to work.

Just then the second match burned out, and Jimmy and his father were plunged into complete darkness.

"Light another match, Father!" Jimmy nearly shouted. Unable to hide his terror as the image of the horrible painting burned in his mind, he seized his father's arm.

"Ahhh!" his father screamed, fumbling for the matches, quickly shaking one out, and lighting it as fast as he could. "You scared me, boy!" He pulled the whiskey from his pocket. "Maybe I just need a little drink to calm my nerves."

But as he removed the cap, Jimmy stopped him, laying a hand on his father's arm. "Maybe you *don't* need a drink, Father" he said, leveling a serious gaze at the trembling man.

Silently, his father put the bottle back in his pocket. "M-maybe the whiskey's playing games with my imagination," he said with a nervous laugh. He noticed that the match was burning low, so he quickly lit a new one. "Best not to let the darkness sneak up on us again, right, boy?" he added, continuing up the stairs and making a point not to look at any of the other paintings.

At the top of the stairs, a hallway stretched into the distance. Several closed doors stood on one wall, while the opposite side offered an open view of the entry hall and front door on the floor below. Old white candles drooped from tarnished holders on the walls, and Jimmy's father plucked one from its perch. "This'll keep things nice and bright for us," he said as he held the match flame to the wick. "Now, let's see where we might bed down for the night."

"I'll have a look in here," Jimmy said, standing in front of the nearest door.

"That's fine, boy," his father said, walking up behind him. "But I think we should stay together. There might be a ghost in there," he added with a nervous chuckle.

As Jimmy swung the door open, a wave of cold air seemed to burst out of the room and pass through the boy and his father. It was like an icy breeze, and yet the flame of the candle didn't even flicker. And then, just as quickly as it had come, the cold air vanished.

Jimmy looked at his father who was looking at him, but neither said a word. Then, the two quietly stepped into the room.

It was a large bedroom with a huge, intricately-carved four-poster bed in the center. The bed was unmade, and the blankets and sheets where all tangled together as though someone had just been sleeping . . . except for one horrible thing. The sheets were soaked with red, fresh blood!

"Someone's been murd—" But Jimmy's father didn't finish his sentence. For halfway between the word "murdered," the horrific scene before him slowly faded away. Now, the bewildered father and son stared open mouthed at nothing but an old rotting bed, stripped of sheets and blankets. There were several rust-colored stains on the floor, but not a single drop of blood.

"D-did y-you see th-that?" Jimmy stammered.

His father, sure he was having hallucinations from drinking too much, quickly shut his opened mouth and mumbled, "I don't know what you're talking about, boy." Then, trying to still his rapidly beating heart, he strolled into the room. "This looks like a fine place to sleep."

"Father," Jimmy began, wondering if his eyes were playing tricks on him, "there must be other rooms."

But his father had already made up his mind. Not wanting to chance seeing an even worse hallucination—as if that were possible—he unstrapped his bedroll and tossed it to the floor. "Let's rest, boy. It must be close to midnight. We can explore the rest of the house in daylight."

Actually, what Jimmy didn't know was that his father was thinking that, at this point, he'd rather not stay in *any* room in this house. But if he admitted to seeing what he thought he saw, his father knew Jimmy would surely start lecturing him on his drinking.

"What are you standing there for, boy?" his father asked. "Come lay out your roll right beside me." He patted the place on the floor between him and the huge, four-poster bed. "Unless you'd rather sleep up there," he added, nodding toward the rotting, rust-stained mattress.

"No . . . no the floor is fine with me," Jimmy said with a nervous smile. He looked around the room as he began laying out his bedroll next to the old bed. Perhaps it *was* all in his imagination. Everything certainly appeared to be perfectly normal now. He lay down next to his father and looked over at the bed. Although the mattress was clearly ruined, the wood had beautifully-carved faces in it, old-fashioned smiling suns, and little jolly elves.

Surely nothing bad could have happened here, Jimmy thought, not knowing that his father, who had just blown out the candle was thinking the exact same thing.

But as soon as darkness touched the room, a crash boomed overhead, followed by the drumming of furious drops pelting the roof above them. Both Jimmy and his father struggled from their bedrolls. The skies had shown no signs earlier of a rainstorm on the way, and yet the sounds of thunder and pouring water were unmistakable. As the two stood in the dark room staring out the window, Jimmy began to hear something besides the sounds of thunder and rain. At first he wasn't sure what he was hearing, and then he was sure it was the rattling of chains . . . from somewhere far below.

Was there some connection between these noises and the bloody bed? his mind raced. *Could someone have been murdered here during a thunderstorm?*

"Father, can you hear those—" Jimmy began. But the look on his father's face as he raised his hand for silence told Jimmy that his father had heard the chains, too.

Already the man was grabbing his matches and preparing to light the candle.

As the room came to life in the eerie glow of the candle, Jimmy and his father looked around the room in stunned silence. Somehow the eyes carved into the faces on the bed were . . . watching them!

Finally, Jimmy's father broke the silence. "Something terrible happened in this room," he whispered, as the sounds of the chains became louder, clanking on each wooden step as they made their way upstairs. "People were killed in that bed, years and years ago, and now, for some reason, the whole terrible thing is about to happen again." He stared, wild-eyed, at his son who hadn't said a word. The chains were now dragging down the hall—toward the bedroom. "Boy! We have to get out of here!" he screamed.

For a moment, Jimmy hesitated as he caught sight of himself in the cracked mirror across from the bed. His image appeared normal . . . except that he had no head!

"Ahhhh!" Jimmy screamed. Grabbing his bedroll and bolting for the window that his father was struggling to open, he pushed his father aside and smashed the glass with the bedroll wrapped around his wrist. Then both he and his father stood there unable to believe what they were seeing. The storm that raged outside did not go farther than the grounds around the house. In fact, it was the house *alone* that the eye of the storm seemed to be focused upon.

Jimmy's father leaned over the windowsill. It was a long way down. Then he saw the trellis, covered with twisted vines of long-dead ivy. "Climb down that trellis!" he yelled at his son, a no-nonsense tone in his voice.

"Hurry, boy!" he shrieked as the chains began pounding on the bedroom door.

Jimmy scrambled out the window, the weathered wood of the old trellis creaking under his weight. Waiting anxiously, his father watched the boy's slow descent, until the bedroom door crashed open and the chains entered the room, and like metal snakes, rattled toward the window.

"I'm right behind you, Jimmy!" his father called, climbing out onto the window sill.

But the moment he put his full weight onto the unsteady trellis, it ripped away from the house in a cloud of splinters, and suddenly both Jimmy and his father were flying to the ground.

"Are you all right, Father?" Jimmy asked, rolling over in the thick covering of snow that had padded his landing.

His father groaned and nodded. "Come on, boy. Let's get away from here."

The two rose slowly and trudged away from the house toward the dark forest. Jimmy didn't even bother to look back at the house, but his father did. If the boy had, he would have been just as awestruck as his father, who saw that the house was no longer plagued by the thunderstorm, and the window Jimmy had broken had miraculously repaired itself.

For awhile, the two walked in silence, then finally they stopped to rest. Brushing the snow off an old log for himself and his father, Jimmy sat down and looked at the old man, who seemed to have aged a full decade.

"Father, may I ask you something?" he said, his breath coming out in frosty puff of air. "Did you see everything I just saw back at that house?"

Jimmy's father locked eyes with his son under the cold moonlight. "I didn't see a thing," he murmured. Then, as if to make a point, he reached into his pocket and grabbed his whiskey bottle. For a second, Jimmy was afraid his father was going to take a drink. But instead, the man tossed the bottle into the woods, where it shattered on a large boulder.

"I'll have no more of that," his father said quietly. "I always told myself I'd quit for good if I ever started seeing things."

After resting a few minutes, the two stood again. It was too cold to remain still for long, and Jimmy was glad to be walking again. For a moment, he stopped and looked back to see if he could catch a glimpse of the terrible old house. Had he really seen and heard all that he'd thought he had? Or had his father's hallucinations somehow triggered his own imagination?

Shrugging, the boy turned and trudged along after the old man, knowing that the wolves might be on them again before the night was over. But somehow Jimmy wasn't as afraid as he had been before. In fact, he wasn't particularly afraid of anything he faced in his future any more. For now that his father had stopped drinking, so much seemed possible.

PLANTING THE YARD – 1914

Michael stared at the land surrounding the crumbling mansion. "It's hopeless, Mr. Pearce," he said, shaking his head. "Nothing will grow in this earth."

The moment he spoke, Michael knew he should have known better. Mr. Pearce frowned, grabbed him by the shoulders and moved so close that their noses almost touched. Michael shuddered. Mr. Pearce's thick glasses made his eyes look as big as hard-boiled eggs, and the old man's breath smelled like rotten eggs as he spoke.

"We've been paid to plant this yard, Michael, and plant it we will!" he barked, his curly white hair clinging to his head like a wispy cloud. "That's what gardeners *do*. Or have you changed your mind about being my apprentice?"

"No sir, Mr. Pearce," Michael said. "I *want* to learn how to plant. I want to learn everything about gardening."

It was the truth. Twelve-year old Michael Carrington had loved plants and growing things ever since he could lift a hoe. He'd been overjoyed when he'd landed this job for the summer, even though the hours were long and Mr. Pearce was as stubborn and difficult as any man he'd ever met. Still, he'd already learned a lot from the old gardener. But somehow Michael was afraid of working at this place, and now, as he looked at the black soil that surrounded it, he wondered if even Mr. Pearce could get anything to grow there. The man was a professional, but he couldn't work miracles.

"Let's get the spades," Mr. Pearce said. "I want the area by this brick walkway finished by sundown." He nodded toward the dark Victorian mansion standing in the exact center of the lifeless area. "Who knows? A few colorful flowers might even dress up an ugly old lady like that."

Their horse-drawn wagon filled with gardening tools and tiny pots of flowers was parked up on the side of the road. Mr. Pearce marched them back to it at a sharp clip. They quickly selected the tools they needed and brought them back to the jumbled bricks that made up the long walkway in front of the mansion. The original gardeners had laid borders for nice wide flower beds along each side of the walk.

"You take the left side and I'll take the right," Mr. Pearce ordered. They began, kneeling and breaking up the clay beneath them a bit at a time, then blending in fertilizer and nutrients, edging a little closer each time to the sagging front porch.

To Michael the dark mansion looked indescribably ancient. It was ugly, too, in the same sickening way that something dead is ugly. The place had fallen into ruin, and the present owners wanted it fixed up to sell. Michael didn't envy the carpenters who would be called to repair the house once they were through with the yard. Something about the lonely structure made him want to look away every time he caught sight of it.

For the remaining hours of the morning, he and Mr. Pearce tilled the foul-smelling soil. Then all afternoon they planted. By dusk, rows of freshly-watered petunias and marigolds lined the walk, and the two gardeners, young and old, stepped back to admire their work.

"Looks better, doesn't it?" Mr. Pearce asked, rubbing the dust from his thick glasses with one of his shirttails.

Michael nodded uneasily, then followed his boss up to the wagon to head for home. He could not keep from casting a last nervous glance back at the mansion. Although he knew the old place had been deserted for years, all day he had had the strangest feeling that they were being watched out of the mansion's dull black windows.

At sunup the next morning Mr. Pearce's old nag towed the wagon back to its resting place at the side of the road. Mr. Pearce had brought a plow today for them to break up the land for grassseed. But as soon as they pulled up, Michael noticed something strange. "Mr. Pearce . . ." he said, his voice a whisper, nodding toward the brick walkway.

The old man turned and looked where the boy had indicated. "Well, would you look at that," he gasped, staring openmouthed at the brick walkway, now touched by the long shadows of the rising sun. The flowers alongside the walk were drab, no longer bright and beautiful as they had been just the day before. "Come on, Michael," he said, practically leaping out of the wagon. "Let's have a look."

Michael jogged behind the old man toward the scene of their previous day's labors. Neither could make any sense out of what they saw.

Each flower head had been neatly lopped off. And there was something else as well. The soil, which they'd left yesterday looking moist and rich, was dead again, squeezing the stem of each headless flower like drying cement.

Mr. Pearce was speechless, at first. Then his glasses clouded over with the steam of his angry breath as he muttered through clenched teeth, "This ground was drier than I thought." He looked straight at the old house as if accepting a challenge. "We'll just do it again," he added, and he turned on his heel and marched back to the wagon. "Mark my words, Michael. We'll not leave this yard until it's been properly planted."

Without a word, Michael followed the old man, and together the two harnessed the old horse to the plow. Then, while Mr. Pearce prodded the animal on behind the plow, Michael ran before it, prying large stones out of the way with a firm metal rod.

They worked in total silence for several hours. And although Michael was busy trying to please his boss, he stopped every so often to glance up at the foreboding mansion. As usual he was unable to look for long. It was as though the old house called him into a staring contest— his eyes versus the cold, pupilless windows of the mansion. So far, the house always won.

Michael lived a couple of towns over, and knew little of the history of the old estate. He did know that some folks thought it was haunted, and he'd heard that many people had come to call its address—1313 *Wicket* Way—1313 Wicked Way. Now he understood why.

For the rest of the afternoon, they worked the ground nonstop. Then, just when Michael thought the day was over, his relentless boss insisted they plant some small trees at different places about the property. It was as though the man was possessed with work, and it wasn't until almost sunset that he finally agreed to head home.

The next day—which was Friday—Mr. Pearce told Michael they would flatten everything out with a steel drum, then strew the ground with grass seed. "And on Saturday," the man added, "we'll replant the flower beds."

As Michael listened to Mr. Pearce, he noticed that the old gardener was not looking at him. He was staring at the mansion . . . as if he were talking to *it*.

Mr. Pearce was in a good mood the next morning as their horsecart bumped over the potholes in the road. "If we can put in another few days like yesterday, we'll have this job wrapped up in no time," he said happily.

Michael nodded. He wished that this job was already finished, and the closer they got to the mansion, the more uncomfortable he began to feel.

As it turned out, there was a reason for Michael's uneasiness, and the moment they pulled up to the old place, he and Mr. Pearce both felt it tenfold. Once again, the earth they'd toiled over was black and crusted over.

Without exchanging a word, the two jumped down from the cart and stood at the perimeter of the property, unable to comprehend what they were seeing. The trees had been uprooted, and lay in pieces in the center of the land they'd so carefully prepared. But what really sent a trickle of fear down Michael's spine was that the ruined branches had been laid out to form words. Shaking his head in disbelief, Mr. Pearce walked over to read what they said, and Michael followed.

"GO AWAY," the stick-message spelled out. "YOU'LL NEVER PLANT THIS YARD."

"Oh, yes we will!" Mr. Pearce screamed, shaking his fist at the mansion. "Do you hear me? We'll plant this yard if it's the last thing we do!"

"Mr. Pearce . . ." Michael began.

"Don't you see what's been happening, boy?" Mr. Pearce snapped. "There's transients living in that house!"

"But what if it's something worse?" Michael asked, unable to hide the tremor in his voice.

"What *could* be worse?" the old man countered. He stared hard at the dark, brooding place. "There are bums living in there, don't you see? And they're the ones who have been poisoning the ground and vandalizing our good work! They don't want this place sold, because then they'll have no place to live!" He whirled about and yelled again at the house. "Isn't that right?"

The house simply stood there, cold and silent in the middle of the dead land.

"Mr. Pearce, I've been having bad feelings about this place ever since we first came here," Michael confessed. "There's a library in town. Maybe we could read up on it."

But Mr. Pearce wasn't listening. "We ought to go in there and roust them out," he said angrily. Then he snatched a sharp pair of shears from the wagon. "These ought to send 'em running."

To Michael, the thought of entering the horrid old place was unthinkable. He would sooner climb into a lion's den. He had to make Mr. Pearce understand what he felt in his very bones. "Please, Mr. Pearce," he begged. "We could be in worse danger than you think. We shouldn't do anything before we find out about the history of this house."

Mr. Pearce stared at Michael for a second. Then he unhitched the wagon. "Okay, son," he said softly. "If it's that important to you, take the horse into town and read up on the place. I'll wait here in case those cowards decide to come out."

Michael thanked the old man, then mounted the horse. For a moment he looked back at the black yard. All their work had been reduced to a pile of broken trees and a row of headless flowers—by what? This wasn't the kind of thing transients would do. "Just promise me one thing, Mr. Pearce," he said as he prepared to ride off. "Promise me you won't go into that house."

The old man grinned. "I'll promise you this. If you're not back here in one hour, I'm *definitely* going in."

Not wasting another moment, Michael kicked the horse and took off at a gallop. The town of Creighton was two miles away, and he wanted to have as much time at the library as possible.

Fifteen minutes later, Michael trotted up to a private home on the town's main street. Outside was a crudely painted sign that read "Town Library." He tied the horse to a post, bounded up the porch steps, and knocked on the front door. After a few moments, an old woman with long gray hair appeared.

"I've got to get some information about the mansion at 1313 Wicket Way," Michael said urgently.

The old woman's eyes grew wide. "One moment, please," she said, then swiftly closed the door.

Michael paced back and forth on the porch, peering now and then at the stacks of books and old newspapers he could see behind a crack in the curtains. *Why couldn't she just let me in?* he wondered, worrying about how much of his hour had already gone by.

Finally, the old woman, wearing a pink bathrobe and slippers, opened the door. Dusty books rose on shelves behind her. "Now, what was it you wanted to know about the old Jardine place?" she asked in a crabby voice.

"Well, I've heard it's supposed to be haunted," Michael began, "and I've come here to—"

The old woman let out a little cackle. "I suppose if you believe in that nonsense, you'll find something to fuel your imagination in there." She gestured to a smaller room to her right. "That's where all our really old manuscripts are." She waved him on, and turned to leave. "Now you be careful and don't leave a mess. I'm going back to bed."

Michael thanked her and hurried into the cramped room. There he began paging through old yellow newspapers and peeking in books which had lost their covers. The old woman had certainly compiled a large amount of historical material about the area, but it soon became obvious that organization was not her strong suit.

As time passed, Michael feared that he would find nothing about the dark mansion, at least not in the few minutes he had left before he had to start back. In fact, he was beginning to wonder if there *wasn't* anything unusual about the old house, and that maybe Mr. Pearce had been right about transients causing all the damage.

But they could be dangerous, too, Michael suddenly thought with alarm. And with that he decided he'd better get back before the stubborn old man tried to enter the house alone.

As he stood to leave, his eyes suddenly fell on a file folder he hadn't seen before. It was marked "Jardine Estate," and he quickly began flipping through it.

The first thing he read was a two-column newspaper clipping dated 1798. Three convicts from the local prison had died at the house while it was being built, the story said. Apparently, they'd been brought to the house to lay out the yard as well.

"They were gardeners," Michael gasped, paging from one yellowing newspaper article to another—each headline he read, making his heart beat faster. "Jardine Family Slaughtered," read one. "Strange Disappearances Tied to Jardine Mansion," another screamed off the page.

His hands trembling, Michael tossed the file down. Then wanting to scream, he ran out the door, mounted his horse, and galloped all the way back to the terrible house on the hill. *If the spirits of the original gardeners still lingered at the Jardine mansion, how would they react now that new gardeners had arrived to take over their yard?* his mind raced. *Not well,* he decided. *Perhaps even with murderous vengeance!*

49

Finally the mansion came into sight through the trees, but Michael didn't see Mr. Pearce. He jumped off the horse, his heart thumping, and quickly tethered the heavily breathing animal to a tree. Then he raced off toward where he spotted the wagon.

But as he approached the old wagon, something about it caught his eye. There, on the wooden side, a large, message had been painted in bright red. Michael stopped dead in his tracks and his mouth fell open when he saw that the message was written not in paint, but in blood.

CONGRATULATIONS, MR. PEARCE, the message said, each of its letters dripping and creating pools of red on the ground. YOU'VE FINALLY PLANTED THE YARD!

"Mr. Pearce!" Michael screamed, looking wildly around the yard. But his boss was nowhere to be seen. Finally the boy's eyes locked onto the dark mansion, fifty feet away. Steeling himself, Michael slowly walked toward it. "Mr. Pearce?" he called, his voice quavering as he stepped onto the brick walkway. "Are you in the house?"

But Mr. Pearce was *not* in the mansion—Michael realized that as soon as he'd gone about halfway down the brick walk . . . and stumbled over the old man's glasses. The thick lenses were red and sticky, and at that moment, Michael understood what the message on the wagon actually meant. The yard *had* finally been planted . . . with Mr. Pearce.

The scream building in Michael's throat ever since he'd first seen the terrible mansion finally burst out of him. It echoed in the trees, off the black earth, and all through the Jardine Mansion itself.

Picture This – 1930

Anita Jardine had painted many things in her thirteen years. In fact, she was the kind of artist who could put almost any subject on canvass. She had a feel for realistically shading the muscles of a racing horse, or capturing just the right shine in a puppy's eyes. And she painted portraits of her younger brothers, Kyle and Lyle, that not only looked just like them, but clearly revealed the twins' mischievous personalities as well.

The old mansion at the edge of the forest was the one thing Anita had never tried to capture in her oils, watercolors, or pastels. And the odd thing was, the house had been right in front of her during her entire life. Her bedroom, which also served as her studio, was on the second floor of their home, and from the window she had a clear view of the forest and the horrible mansion which, many years ago, had belonged to her ancestors.

It was an ugly house, and from her bedroom, Anita could see its top windows—all of which peered at her like the eyes of an angry ghost. The mansion had always made her uncomfortable, and whenever she sat at her easel, Anita tried to pretend it wasn't there, and to forget what her mother had told her about the place—that long ago, some of her ancestors had died there. Other relatives claimed they had seen ghosts. And more recently, Anita's own great-grandfather had broken his arm in a piano that still sat in one of the house's rooms.

But as hard as she tried to *not* look at the mansion, Anita often caught herself drawn to it. And often she daydreamed about walking up its rickety staircase and . . .

"This is ridiculous!" Anita scolded herself, as she once again realized that the mansion had enveloped her.

Shaking off the trancelike feeling she had slipped into while staring at the awful place, Anita got up and clipped a fresh canvass to her easel. That morning she had awakened with an overwhelming urge to paint, and that was precisely what she intended to do.

As always, she began by sketching an idea onto the canvass, which she would later paint over. This morning she had a peaceful scene in mind, something with a deer in a forest glade. But as she worked, Anita felt distracted. Earlier, her five-year-old brothers had hidden her oils, and although she'd found them, Anita was still fuming.

She streaked the charcoal in long strokes across the canvass. *Why can't Mother keep them out of my things!* she thought angrily. The truth was, Kyle and Lyle were like tiny whirlwinds, racing through the house and causing havoc wherever they went. But this time they'd gone too far. Her paints were expensive, and if they spilled one drop, Anita would make sure that they both paid dearly.

Despite her foul mood, Anita finally lost herself in the sketch, and before she knew it, she'd created a forest scene. But it wasn't the one she'd meant to create. Instead, what had poured through her fingers was the exact scene that transfixed Anita every day from her window. There was the outline of trees at the forest's edge, with the wispy clouds above. And looming just at the top of the hill was that terrible, grim mansion. Even in a sketched form, it looked so realistic and sinister that the charcoal fell from Anita's fingers at the sight of it.

She wanted to rip the horrible sketch from her easel and destroy it. But instead she just stared at the dark sketch for a few moments, feeling herself drawn to it as she was to the mansion itself. Then, suddenly feeling sick to her stomach, she shuddered and quickly left the room.

As soon as they saw Anita leave, the twins danced into her room. Kyle was carrying the freshly-caught frog they planned to plant somewhere in their sister's things. But as they were scanning the room, the twins suddenly stopped dead when they saw the picture on the easel.

Then, for some reason the fun and mischief seemed to leave the boys like air escaping from a balloon. And for a long time, the brothers simply stood in silence before the easel and the ominous sketch that stood on it.

That afternoon Anita had planned to go horseback-riding with friends, and she was glad that the odd feelings the sketch had instilled in her had not kept her from going.

For when she returned from the carefree ride, Anita felt her cheerful self again. The awful sketch far from her mind, she bounded up the stairs. But the moment she entered her bedroom, she was instantly drawn to her easel.

"This is impossible," she muttered, staring in disbelief. There, in one of the top windows of the mansion, three tiny smudges had been added! It looked like a trio of badly drawn shadow-people standing before the glass.

Those brats! Anita thought, instantly realizing who was to blame. Without thinking about it, she sat down and erased the images with dabs of white paint. "There, that's better," she murmured, as if talking to the sketch. She had to admit it was nicely done, even if the subject was unsettling. Perhaps turning the charcoal drawing into a painting wasn't such a bad idea after all, especially since she'd never before abandoned a sketch that had as much promise as this one. And so, with a sigh of resolve, Anita picked up her oils and began, completely forgetting that she'd come upstairs not to paint, but to change her clothes for dinner.

Mixing drab, dark colors, Anita worked until the ancient house was clearly pictured, from its black chimney down to the warped boards of its trim. The image of the rotting house was such a familiar sight in her life that she felt no need to even look out the window at her subject as she painted fast and furiously. So fast, that before her mother called her down to supper, she had nearly finished the entire piece. Amazed, she paused to study her work and was startled at how alive the house seemed.

Feeling a sudden chill, she rose to shut the open window, when she heard a muffled noise. Her heart throbbing, Anita scanned the room, trying to figure out what the noise was and where it was coming from. As if in a dream, she walked slowly toward the sound, which she now realized was coming from her bed. And now, in horror, she saw that the sheets were moving!

In one swift move she threw the covers back . . . and screamed as a frog leapt out from the linens.

Instantly, the room filled with laughter and Anita's tormentors, Kyle and Lyle, burst through the door.

"Father has just come home!" Kyle sang out.

"And Mother wants you at dinner!" Lyle added.

Then they both turned and ran from the room, their breathless giggles echoing down the hall.

That night Anita dreamed she was in a gloomy place where the air smelled of mold and dust. Laughter echoed everywhere. At first she thought it was her brothers up to more mischief, but as she searched the darkness for their faces, she saw nothing. Slowly Anita realized that it couldn't be the fun-loving giggles of Kyle and Lyle. No, this laugher was of grown men, raspy and deep.

Her forehead beaded with perspiration, Anita woke with a start and looked about her room. "It was only a dream," she whispered aloud, relieved to see all her familiar things. For a few moments she lay there, trying to relax. But soon, realizing that there was no way she'd be able to get back to sleep, she decided to get up and paint. Flicking on her bedside light, Anita glanced over at her easel, and her mouth fell open. She couldn't believe it. Her brothers had changed her picture again!

Angrily throwing off her covers, she stormed over to the painting, then stopped dead in her tracks. Kyle's and Lyle's artwork was actually improving. In fact, it looked nearly professional. There, next to the front door of the crumbling house, were three human shapes, looking as if they'd just walked out onto the porch. She looked closer, feeling goosebumps rising on the back of her arms. Obviously the twins had mixed too much water in with the paint, for the three figures looked strangely transparent, almost ghostly. She could see the gray front door of the mansion right through them.

"Those little monsters," Anita grumbled, as she grabbed a brush and dabbed over the eerie forms on the doorstep. As she worked her hands shook, and she grew so cold that she began shivering so severely that she had to crawl back into bed once she was done.

But as she lay there, trying to get some warmth back into her body, Anita had to admit to herself that perhaps it wasn't the cold, damp air of the early hour that was giving her the chills. For in the back of her mind a disturbing question continued to gnaw at her: *What if her brothers had nothing at all to do with the picture changing?* She shivered and burrowed deeply under her comforter. What if the picture was changing by itself?

For the rest of the night, Anita hardly slept a wink, and the next morning she marched downstairs to the breakfast table to confront her brothers.

"All right!" she yelled. "Which one of you has been messing around with my painting?"

Kyle and Lyle looked at her innocently. Then they glanced quickly at each other and shrugged.

"What's all this about?" asked their mother, standing before the stove. She turned to stare sternly at the boys. "Are you two up to something again?"

"They're drawing things on my painting!" Anita cried, scarcely able to contain her temper.

"We didn't!" Kyle protested.

"We were too scared to go near it," Lyle admitted.

"So you were in her room," their mother said, wagging a finger at the boys. Then she turned to Anita and smiled. "I'm taking your brothers into downtown Creighton all day to do the week's shopping," she said. "So you should at least have a peaceful day." Heaving a tired sigh, she walked over to her sons and put a firm hand on each of their shoulders. "Your sister's room is off limits to both of you," she said firmly. "Do you understand me?"

The two boys nodded—both at the same time.

Later, Anita headed back upstairs. She was bothered by what the twins said about being scared of her painting. The truth was, she too felt frightened whenever she looked at it.

Of course, that was ridiculous. It was, after all, merely a picture, and one that she herself was painting. Yet now, as she entered her room, Anita found herself hesitating before she walked over to her easel. *What if the picture had changed again during the time she was at breakfast?* she thought frantically. *Then it couldn't have been the twins who were responsible.*

As if not wanting to disturb someone who was sound asleep, Anita carefully tiptoed across the floor toward the canvass. *I'm just being silly,* she told herself. *There's nothing to be afraid of.* And with that she reached out and yanked off the cloth she had thrown over the painting during the night . . . and screamed.

The three figures were back. They now stood in the forest near the stump of a tree which had been hit by lightening. As before, the three men were rendered with a thin mix of paint so that Anita could see the trees right through their bodies. The details of their faces were indistinct, but now they clearly were wearing old-fashioned prison uniforms. And there was something else. The trio was larger this time—as if they'd been moving closer . . . toward *Anita's* house!

Anita threw the cloth back over the picture and sat down on her bed, trembling from head to toe. "Who is doing this?" she moaned aloud. "And what do they want?"

Suddenly she had the strongest urge to look out the window. What if the three ghostly figures existed. What if they really had left the old house and were making their way toward her . . . this very moment? She stood quickly, before she could give herself time to think about it, and strode over to the window.

The view was the same as ever, except now, among all the trees in the forest, was the blackened stump of a tree that had been hit by lightening. It was the same one the prisoners had been standing next to in the picture!

On an impulse, Anita ran out of the house. Maybe the stump held some clues as to what was happening.

Outside, the sky had clouded over, so the forest was darker than usual. Making her way through the scraggly manzanita bushes and through clusters of pines, Anita finally found the charred stump. Examining it closely, she could tell that the tree hadn't been struck too long ago, for there were still fresh piles of ash on either side of what was left of it. Then Anita saw something that made her heart freeze. Imprinted plainly in the ashes were several large footprints.

"Somebody *has* been here!" she cried. She stared in terror at the direction the prints had taken, winding through the trees . . . right toward her house!

A dull booming grumbled from the skies, reminding Anita this was thunderstorm season. She knew she had to hurry home, yet home was the last place she wanted to be right now. But where else was there to go? She stood up on the burnt stump, and looked around the forest frantically. There was nothing but trees to shelter her from the brewing storm—nothing except for the dark mansion in the near distance, the dark mansion that now seemed to be calling her, *willing* her to come to it.

A cold wind whipped through the trees, chilling Anita to the bone as she fought her urge to go to the mansion. It was as if it *needed* her to come to it, needed to tell her its story. She'd already heard so many terrible things about the horrible place. She'd heard all the stories about how it was haunted by three prisoners who her great-great grandfather hired to build it, three prisoners who had died in a thunderstorm in the mansion's basement. *Could the three angry spirits still be looking to avenge their deaths?* she wondered. *And was this thunderstorm that threatened now somehow giving them the power to return?*

Trying not to panic, Anita suddenly realized a way to break the mansion's control over her. It was the painting! Filled with sudden hope, she began running toward her house. If she could destroy the picture before it depicted the spirits entering her house, perhaps the spell would be broken!

Just then a thunderbolt cracked through the clouds and struck somewhere in the forest. Anita knew that a downpour could not be far behind. Running like fear itself was propelling her, Anita practically flew toward her house, and she reached the front porch just as the first fat drops of rain fell from the black sky.

Had she beaten them? Anita wondered. Throwing open the door, Anita stood there panting for a moment, listening for some sign of the ghostly prisoners. Satisfied that she was alone, she raced to the fireplace, laid out a pile of kindling and wood, then lit it. She had to build a good strong fire, one powerful enough to consume her painting and destroy it not only quickly but completely.

What will happen when I put the picture in the fire? she thought, poking the embers as they slowly began to flame. *Will I hear horrid shrieks of the spirits as the fire destroys the canvass?*

Deciding that the fire was well underway, Anita rose, and on trembling legs, she walked up the stairs to her bedroom. She had to get the picture now, before it was too late. She had to destroy the canvass before it showed the prisoners inside the house.

As she ascended the stairs, the rain outside grew louder, and soon it was drumming hard on the roof. With each crack of thunder she nearly jumped out of her skin, but still she pressed on until finally she entered her room. There was the picture, still covered by the cloth exactly as she'd left it. But *had* it changed? Were the images of the prisoners *inside* her house now?

"I'm not looking," she told herself. "I'm just going to leave it covered, pick it up, and take it downstairs."

Slowly, Anita crept toward the easel, but before she could reach it, the cloth slipped off the canvass completely of its own accord.

"No!" Anita cried, her eyes nearly bugging out of her head at what she saw. The entire perspective of the picture had changed. Now the terrible mansion was in the distance, and the painting was focused on the closeup of a window . . . *her* window! And there was a dark figure climbing through it!

Anita couldn't bear to look at her real window. All she could do was listen to the voice in her head chanting, *Paint over it. Paint over it. Paint over it.*

Completely forgetting her plan to throw the canvass in the fire, Anita lunged for one of her paintbrushes. Then without caring which colors she used, she painted large splotches all over the picture, trying to cover the hideous image with as much paint as she could.

But as the brush continued to swipe at the canvass, Anita suddenly felt it jerk in her fingers. She tried to drop the brush, but somehow her fingers tightened their grip around it . . . as it slowly began to pull her *into* the painting itself.

"Help! Anita shrieked as her hand, then her entire arm disappeared into the canvass. "Someone, please help me!"

Suddenly a cruel laughter filled her ears. It was the same laughter that had been in her dream.

By the time their mother brought Kyle and Lyle home, the storm was over. A huge fire raged in the fireplace, but Anita was not sitting by it reading, nor was she napping in front of it in a peaceful sleep.

"Go find your sister," Anita's mother told the twins. "Tell her to come look at her lovely new dress you helped pick out."

Giggling with excitement, the boys stomped up the stairs, and raced into Anita's room. "Anita's not here!" Kyle called over his shoulder.

"Yeah, but it looks like she's finished her painting!" Lyle shouted.

Together the boys walked to the easel and stared at the colorful forest, dark blue sky, and stark mansion nestled in the trees.

"Hey, look at that," Kyle said, pointing to one of the windows. "Anita's painted *herself* in the picture!"

"Yeah," Lyle murmured. "It looks just like her, too."

The twins crowded closer to the picture, staring at a window high in the mansion, where a tiny image of their sister stared miserably out of the glass with eyes full of sadness and fear.

BOARD GAME — 1931

Mary Beth Hollingsworth wasn't looking forward to her cousin coming to spend the summer. Lizzy was ten, an entire two years younger than Mary Beth, and entertaining her for three months sounded like the most boring thing Mary Beth could imagine.

But Lizzy turned out to be anything but boring. In fact, within two hours of her arrival, she cornered Mary Beth in her bedroom with an interesting proposition.

"Want to see a real spook board?" she asked.

Before Mary Beth could even ask what a spook board was, the younger girl had unsnapped her suitcase and revealed a polished wooden board. Strange designs, an alphabet, the numbers one through ten, and the words YES and NO had all been hand-burned onto its surface.

"This is a Ouija board," Lizzy explained, seeing Mary Beth's confusion. "By sliding this thing called a planchette across the board," she said, holding up a heart-shaped ivory pointer, "we can contact spirits of dead people."

Mary Beth suppressed a shudder that ran through her body. "That sounds like fun," she murmured, feeling excited and fearful all at once. "Who should we contact?"

"Well, I've heard rumors about that haunted house in your neighborhood," Lizzy said, a finger twirling her long braid of hair. "I bet someone died in there."

Mary Beth studied the strange-looking board. "Sure. Let's give it a try," she said, filled with curiosity. "How about tonight after my parents are in bed?"

Lizzy nodded eagerly. "Perfect," she said.

Mary Beth's parents closed their bedroom door just after ten, and within minutes, the two cousins sat on Mary Beth's bed and set the polished board between them.

Now examining the board even more closely, Mary Beth saw pictures of suns and moons with dark, scary expressions on them. "Where did you get this?" she asked.

"My grandpa," Lizzy replied. "He likes spooky things, just like I do." She carefully unwrapped the carved ivory pointer and set it on the board. "Now, we're supposed to balance the board between our laps, then put our finger-tips lightly on the pointer."

They did this. "Now what?" Mary Beth asked in a small voice. The darkened room and the weird drawings on the board were starting to make her feel uneasy.

"Well, we ask questions," Lizzy replied. "Then if we actually contact a spirit, the pointer will spell out answers. Got it?"

Mary Beth nodded. She thought of the shadowy Jardine mansion, only a half-mile away, and her stomach twisted. What if they did contact a spirit from that horrid old place? Would they be able to make it go away? She was about to tell her cousin that she didn't think this was such a good idea, when she saw the determined look in Lizzy's eyes.

"Go ahead and ask a question," Mary Beth said, her fingers trembling as she rested them on the ivory pointer.

"Okay, I'd like to know if there are any spirits who would like to talk to us?" Lizzy whispered ominously.

Almost instantly, the pointer on the board started gliding slowly about, seemingly guided by their finger-tips. It went to the word YES, then stopped.

"You moved it!" Mary Beth accused, taking her fingers dramatically off the pointer.

Lizzy looked shocked. "I didn't!" she cried indignantly. "If you don't believe me, why don't *you* ask the question."

Mary Beth hesitantly placed her hands back on the pointer. "All right, spirit," Mary Beth said half-heartedly. "If you are here, identify yourself."

Again the pointer began traveling around the board, stopping briefly at a letter, then jerking into life again. It was obvious to Mary Beth that Lizzy was behind it, but still she had to play along. And then she realized just what was being spelled out on the board, and her skin crawled from head to toe.

The pointer had paused at the letters M and B, then it went on to spell I-T-I-S-A-N-I-T-A.

"There!" Lizzy said triumphantly. "Anyone named 'Anita' ever die around here?"

Mary Beth couldn't answer at first, and when she did, her voice was hoarse. "Anita Jardine was my best friend. She lived about a quarter mile from here and disappeared from her house about six months ago." Her voice cracked. "Anita wanted to be an artist when she grew up."

For a moment Mary Beth stared at the board with a whole new respect. There was no way Lizzy could have known that Anita used to call her "M.B."

"Wasn't the haunted house owned by the Jardine's?" Lizzy asked, her eyes wide.

Mary Beth paused. "Yes, it was passed down from her great-grandfather, but Lizzy and her family never lived in it. The old Jardine mansion was a wreck, and probably still is."

"Have you ever been in it?" Lizzy asked excitedly. "I heard it was on a street called Wicked Way. Is that true?"

Mary Beth laughed. "No, it's actually on *Wicket* Way, but because of all the death surrounding the place, the locals sort of changed the name."

"Come on, put your fingers back on the pointer," Lizzy said eagerly. "I've got another question."

Feeling a little uneasy and not sure if she wanted to keep playing with the board, Mary Beth reluctantly complied. Then Lizzy addressed the spirit in a hollow voice. "Anita, are you in the Jardine mansion right now?"

The pointer not only went to the word YES, but then it spelled out H-E-L-P-M-E-M-B.

Mary Beth's hands were shaking so badly that she could no longer rest her fingertips on the pointer. All she could do was stare at the board in horror. "If this thing only contacts dead people," she whispered, "then that means *Anita* is dead."

Lizzy squirmed. "I think so," she replied softly as she nervously fingered her braid.

And then a wild idea struck Mary Beth. "Lizzy, what if my friend *isn't* dead? What if Anita was running away from something, decided to hide in the old mansion, and somehow got trapped in there?"

Lizzy's face clouded over with thought. "I guess it's possible," she said. "Maybe she fell through a rotting floor board or something."

"Yes!" Mary Beth said excitedly. "And now, maybe she's found a way to communicate with us by using the Ouija board. Maybe we can actually save her!"

Quickly both girls laid their fingertips back on the pointer. "Anita—what should we do?" Mary Beth asked.

The pointer glided under their fingers. C-O-M-E-T-O-T-H-E-A-T-T-I-C, it spelled. H-U-R-R-Y-M-B-I-N-E-E-D-Y-O-U.

This was more than Mary Beth bargained for. She faced her cousin. "B-but it's the middle of the night?" she stammered. "I don't want to go into that creepy old place even during the day. Besides, maybe we should wait until morning and tell my parents."

Lizzy rolled her eyes. "Do you honestly think they're going to believe in a spook board? All they'll do is take it away from us."

For a moment Mary Beth thought of the last time she'd seen Anita. It had been at a birthday party and Anita had given the birthday girl one of her own paintings. Everyone missed Anita so, and now here was a chance to get her back. Mary Beth knew she couldn't let her friend down. Slowly she stood up and looked Lizzy firmly in the eyes. "Let's go," she said with resolve. "Right now."

Everything happened quickly after that. The girls quietly found a flashlight, and Lizzy slipped her Ouija board into its fancy carrying case. Within minutes, they had dressed and were stepping out into the moonlit night.

With the comfort of her own house behind her, Mary Beth now studied the dark trees before them. There were at least three paths leading out of her backyard into the forest, but which one would lead them to Wicket Way. Although she'd lived here all her life, Mary Beth had never once tried to cut through the forest to get to the Jardine mansion, and with good reason. Everyone from her parents to her friends had warned her about the strange things that had happened in that house. She could hardly believe that she was now heading toward it on purpose.

"I—I don't know which path leads to the house," she said nervously to Lizzy.

For a moment the two cousins considered which way to go, then finally settled on the path toward the left. It looped down and around an endless procession of hills and gullies, leading the girls past huge gnarled pine trees and oaks dripping with moss. Finally, after they'd hiked for over half an hour, Mary Beth had convinced herself that they'd taken the wrong trail. She was about to suggest they turn back when they came upon a little rise. At the top, all the trees fell away below them, and there, in the center of a wide, barren meadow, stood the decrepit-looking mansion. Moonlight seemed unable to penetrate its utter blackness, making it look like a bottle of ink in the shape of a house. Both girls stopped walking and stared in silence.

"It really looks haunted, doesn't it?" Lizzy gasped. Mary Beth nodded, then Lizzy added, "My grandfather says you can get a feeling about these things, and that's the feeling I have now."

Mary Beth glanced at her watch. When she saw it was almost midnight, she felt her stomach roll. On a normal night she'd have been sound asleep for hours by now—instead, here they were standing at the edge of a cold forest, planning to enter one of the scariest looking places she'd ever seen.

She took a step, entering the meadow, and Lizzy followed. It might as well have been the surface of the moon, it was so barren, and as the girls walked along, the dry earth kicked up a terrible choking dust.

Soon, the shadow of the house actually reached out to touch their feet, and the girls stopped to look at the forbidding mansion. It towered before them, in a dark silhouette, while banks of high clouds, pushed by the rising wind, rushed behind the outline of its crumbling chimney and roof peaks.

It almost looks alive, Mary Beth thought, as the house crouched before them in the night, making her feel like it might actually awaken with a start and howl at them.

Quietly, the girls crept up to the front porch. Lizzy tried the door, but it didn't budge, so they made their way to the back and found another door. This time Mary Beth reached out and seized the knob. It was cold and oily, and she felt as if she'd touched a frozen bone. "Locked," she whispered, wiping her hand on her jeans.

"Let's ask the Ouija board how to get inside," Lizzy suggested, gesturing for Mary Beth to follow her out into the meadow.

Mary Beth followed her cousin, and soon the two sat across from each other on the cracked earth, the Ouija board balanced on their knees.

Lizzy set the pointer in the middle of the board, and both girls laid their fingertips lightly upon it. "Anita, we want to help you," Mary Beth said. "But you need to tell us how we can we get into the house."

For a moment the only sound was the breathing of the wind, blowing across the meadow. Then a lonely skittering sound came from the board as the pointer began moving beneath their fingers. It pointed out eighteen letters, then stopped abruptly. In her head, Mary Beth separated the message into words. "It spelled out 'stained-glass window,'" she reported.

"I saw one as we were coming around the side of the house!" Lizzy exclaimed. With that she quickly packed away the board and the two hurried over to look.

Sure enough, a long stained-glass window decorated the far side of the mansion. It stood about four feet off the ground, and neither girl could quite make out the design. In the dim moonlight all they could see was several shades of red glass cut at sharp angles.

Slowly, Lizzy reached up to touch the pane, and to her surprise, the wooden window frame swung inward.

"We're in luck," Lizzy whispered excitedly. "Give me a boost."

She laid the board on the ground, then stepped into her cousin's laced fingers. Meanwhile, Mary Beth couldn't help marveling at Lizzy. Though she was only ten years old, Lizzy was definitely the bravest person Mary Beth had ever met. "Are you all right?" she called, once Lizzy had successfully climbed inside.

"I'm okay," Lizzy whispered. "First give me the board and your flashlight. Then I'll give you a hand up."

Outside alone, Mary Beth paused to look up at the dark mansion towering above her. To her, it looked more like a beast, slumbering in the night. When would it awaken? Then remembering that her friend Anita needed her, she shook off her fears, grabbed Lizzy's outstretched hand, and scrambled through the window.

Inside, things smelled stale and dusty, and in the flashlight's faint glow, all the girls could see was the dark angle of a staircase. Suddenly Lizzy whispered into her ear, "We'd better contact Anita for advice."

Startled, Mary Beth jumped, but managed not to let out the shriek that rose in her throat. Who knew what spirits might have heard her?

"Okay," she whispered back, then sat across from Lizzy on the buckled hardwood floor.

At first Mary Beth didn't want to even touch the board. With the moonlight coming through the stained glass, it was lit up in eerie shades of red, like blood. Then deciding that she'd better get this whole thing over with, she gently laid her fingertips on the marker.

"Anita, tell us how to find you?" Lizzy whispered.

"Please, Anita," Mary Beth said. "We want to help you."

The pointer glided quickly about the wooden surface. U-P-S-T-A-I-R-S, it spelled. B-E-Q-U-I-E-T-T-H-E-Y-W-I-L-L-H-E-A-R-Y-O-U-A-N-D-D-O-N-O-T-T-O-U-C-H-T-H-E-T-H-I-R-D-S-T-E-P.

They? Mary Beth thought. She scanned the shadows uneasily. *Does she mean ghosts?*

Suddenly Lizzy touched her arm and Mary Beth nearly tossed the board off their laps and fled from the house.

"Come on," Lizzy whispered. "Let's go find your friend."

Trying to calm her jagged nerves, Mary Beth and Lizzy packed up the board, then taking it with them, the two silently crept toward the rickety-looking staircase.

Lizzy went first, moving as slow as a cat up the warped wooden steps. When it was Mary Beth's turn, she almost forgot about avoiding the third step, but at the last instant, she jumped, making her foot land on the stair just above. After that she moved slower than a snail, terrified that a sudden squeak would give her away.

On the second floor, the cousins seemed to be in a hallway. They knelt near a small window and set up the board again. "Which direction, Anita?" Lizzy whispered.

T-H-E-A-T-T-I-C-L-A-D-D-E-R-I-S-R-I-G-H-T-B-E-H-I-N-D-Y-O-U, spelled the board.

Mary Beth twisted to look for the ladder in the gloom, and as she did, the pointer slid off the Ouija board, hitting the hardwood floor with a loud clatter. "Sorry," she whispered, then quickly replaced the pointer.

Suddenly both girls heard a menacing sound—like chains rattling—coming from somewhere on the lower floor, maybe even *beneath* the house. Then, all at once, though no one had asked a question and neither Mary Beth or Lizzy even had their hands on the pointer, it started to spell something out.

T-H-E-Y-A-R-E-C-O-M-I-N-G-S-T-A-Y-W-H-E-R-E-Y-O-U-A-R-E, the board warned.

Mary Beth tensed as the rattling chains grew louder. It appeared like they were coming up another set of steps below the staircase she and Lizzy had just ascended. *Maybe from the basement,* Mary Beth thought, as the clinking sound of each rusty link hit the first landing.

And now they were coming up the stairs to the second floor! Mary Beth held her breath. The sound had stopped not more than a few feet away from them.

Suddenly a door flew open behind the terrified girls, the metal chains clanked into the room, then the door squeaked closed again. As sounds of screams came from inside, the Ouija board sprang into life. G-O-U-P-T-H-E-L-A-D-D-E-R, it ordered. N-O-W.

Tense with fear, the girls quickly packed up the board as quietly as they could, then scrambled up the wooden rungs.

"It's pitch black up here," Lizzy whispered, wiping a gooey spiderweb from her face. "Turn on the flashlight."

Mary Beth clicked on the beam. "Anita, where are you?" she called quietly.

There was no answer. All that could be heard was the awful sounds of anguish coming from the room below.

"Maybe your friend can only communicate through the board," Lizzy said, quickly taking out the board.

Mary Beth sat down across from Lizzy. "Okay, Anita. We're here. Where are you?"

I-N-T-H-E-C-O-R-N-E-R, the pointer spelled out. A-N-D-D-O-N-O-T-B-E-S-C-A-R-E-D-A-T-W-H-A-T-Y-O-U-S-E-E.

Believing she couldn't possibly be more scared than she already was, Mary Beth shined the flashlight around the attic. The beam fell on ancient boxes and trunks, but their was no sign of Anita.

"Hey, shine the light over there," Lizzy said, gesturing to the right where the ceiling sloped down.

Mary Beth did as she was told, then she and Lizzy crept in the direction of the light . . . until the beam fell on a shape on the floor. Instantly Mary Beth started to scream, but Lizzy clapped a hand over her mouth.

"Is that your friend?" Lizzy asked,

They stared down at Anita's lifeless body, curled into a little ball on a mound of old burlap sacks.

Mary Beth turned away, tears filling her eyes. "I—I was sure she would be alive," she whispered sadly. "Why would a dead person need our help?"

Lizzy put her arm around Mary Beth's shoulders. "I think I know," she said gently. "But let's find out for sure."

As they walked back to the board, Mary Beth realized that the screams echoing through the house were now silent. Slumping dejectedly to the floor across from her cousin, she carefully placed her finger-tips on the pointer. "Why did you call us?" Lizzy asked.

I-C-A-N-N-O-T-R-E-S-T-U-N-T-I-L-M-Y-B-O-D-Y-I-S-B-U-R-I-E-D, the spirit of Anita answered.

Mary Beth looked about the old gloomy room. She now knew what Anita wanted, and that somehow her spirit was somewhere in here watching, waiting for an answer.

Mary Beth stood and walked back to the corner. The idea of touching Anita's corpse made her feel sick, yet if she waited until morning for help with the body, the ghosts might hide Anita in that awful house forever.

Lizzy walked up beside her cousin. "Let's wrap her in the burlap sack," she said bravely.

Mary Beth nodded. Then together, she and Lizzy secured the burlap around the body of her friend.

They were just heading toward the attic ladder, each holding an end of the heavy bundle, when they heard a scratching in the dark.

Her heart pounding wildly, Mary Beth stabbed the flashlight beam in the direction of the sound. It was the Ouija board. They'd forgotten all about it, and the pointer was moving all by itself. For a moment, the girls set down Anita's body and stared at the message in fascination. It had spelled out, T-H-A-N-K-Y-O-U-M-B-A-N-D-C-O-U-S-I-N-L-I-Z-Z-Y.

Now remembering to take the board with them, the girls picked up their burden and descended the ladder. All the while they strained to hear the sounds of the murderous spirits returning, but apparently the terrible ghosts had wreaked their havoc for the night.

Breathing hard under the weight of Anita, Mary Beth and Lizzy now headed down the staircase toward the first floor. But in her haste to get out of the dreaded place, Mary Beth forgot all about the third step—until her foot landed on it.

Instantly the stair creaked loudly, sounding like a screaming animal, and within seconds the clatter of the terrible chains returned.

"Run!" Lizzy shrieked.

They hurried down the rest of the stairs, then bumping into rotting furniture on the first floor, the cousins finally reached the window. Mary Beth pushed through first, and with Lizzy's help, she took Anita's sack-covered body with her. Then she turned to help Lizzy down. As she did, Mary Beth's eyes finally focused on what the stained glass window was depicting. It was a picture of three dark figures slashing off the heads of two terrified adults.

"Get out of that house, Lizzy!" Mary Beth screamed, grabbing her cousin's outstretched arms and pulling her outside. Then each grabbing an end of the burlap bundle, the girls struggled as fast as they could across the barren meadow.

But just before they reached the forest, Mary Beth could not resist glancing back at the terrible house. What she saw made her heart freeze. The stained glass window was still open, and three dark shapes the color of charcoal were floating out.

"They're after us!" Mary Beth cried, plunging into the forest with Lizzy and Anita's body in tow.

"Which path do we take back home?" Lizzy called as the three trails appeared before them. "I can't remember which one we took to get here!"

Mary Beth stared in horror. Suddenly, she felt all turned around, and had no idea which path led home. But there wasn't any time to think. "Follow me!" she shouted, lunging down the right path, hoping it was the same one they had taken earlier.

The trail she'd picked led them into a dense growth of trees. Once they'd entered it, the forest seemed to close about them, shutting out the moonlight as if someone had flicked off a light switch. It was so dark, in fact, that their flashlight barely pointed out the trail, and Mary Beth feared they might get lost.

For a while, they stumbled on, dragging the heavy sack between them as the owls hooted from the branches overhead and strange crackling sounds came from the undergrowth. Once, Mary Beth thought she heard the sound of a wolf, far off in the distance. But that, she knew, was impossible. Wolves disappeared from these woods over thirty years ago. Mary Beth was sure, however, that she heard the dim sound of the chains . . . and they were getting closer.

Exhausted, the girls were finally forced to slow down. For a time the terrifying sound of chains grew louder. Then, much to their relief, the noises simply died away.

The cousins stopped, gulping in the sharp nighttime air. "I've heard that ghosts can't stray too far from the place they died," Lizzy gasped. "Maybe they reached their limit."

Still, the girls continued to stagger onward, dragging the sack. And finally, over the next rise, they saw Mary Beth's backyard. They had made it.

Anita's funeral was held the very next day. Mary Beth and Lizzy told everyone they had stumbled across her body while taking a late walk in the woods. The police decided that a drifter had killed her.

Finally, a week after the funeral service, the cousins pulled out the Ouija board again. Mary Beth felt she had to know if her friend's spirit was still troubled. They sat on the floor of Mary Beth's room, the board across their legs, and lightly placed their fingertips on the pointer.

"Anita?" Mary Beth asked. "Are you still out there?"

For a long time, nothing at all happened. The pointer remained completely motionless.

"We did it," Lizzy said, giving Mary Beth a sad little smile. "She must be at rest—"

But suddenly, the pointer began to make jagged movements all over the board. In fact, it moved so wildly that they could hardly keep their hands on it. Twice in its mad circuit the pointer nearly ran right off the edge.

"What's happening?" Mary Beth cried. When Anita had previously "spoken" to them the pointer had moved in a steady, measured way, not at the frenzied pace it was moving now. With increasing dread, the girls tried to decipher the message that was so furiously being spelled out before them.

As the pointer swooped around across the board, bent on delivering its chilling response to a question that was never asked, the girls tried to stop it by removing their fingertips. But somehow the power that had gained control of the board would not release the girls until it was finished. And finally it was.

With tears streaming down their faces, both girls removed their fingertips from the pointer and looked at their hands as though they'd been burned. It would be the last time in their lives that either of them would ever dare use a Ouija board. And it would be the last time they would dare go near the evil house on Wicket Way.

For by the time the pointer had finished spelling out the message it was clear who had sent it.

N-E-X-T-T-I-M-E-Y-O-U-V-I-S-I-T, the message had read, Y-O-U-W-I-L-L-S-T-A-Y-F-O-R-E-V-E-R.

To Steal a Gargoyle – 1956

Sam and his two best friends, Louis and Wally, looked at the rows of horror novels on his shelves, the plaster glow-in-the-dark skulls lining his desktop, and the rubber tarantulas dangling from hooks above his bed. It would be an understatement to say that Sam liked spooky things.

"I think my room needs something," he said to his buddies, and then his eyes brightened. "I've got it! A gargoyle will be the perfect touch. And luckily I know just where to find one."

"What's a gargoyle?" Louis asked.

Sam touched the long, curved scar on his right cheek that he'd gotten from falling off his bicycle a few weeks before. "You'll see," he said mysteriously as he headed for the door.

For a split second, Wally and Louis glanced at each other. Sam's plans often got them into trouble. Still, neither boy wanted to be left out. Sam had cocked his head for them to follow—and, as usual—they did.

Outside, the boys jumped on their bikes and pedaled across town. Soon they turned down a dirt road leading out of town through the dense woods. Louis and Wally smiled at each other in anticipation of the excitement ahead. Every kid in town knew where this road led.

"Almost there," Sam said ominously, as if his friends didn't know perfectly well where they were headed.

As the sky grew dark, blotted out by the gnarled trees above, black crows began cawing wildly from the branches. Wally had to get off and walk his bike. The final hill was a big one and he was a little overweight. But finally the three boys crested the hill, and together they stood there looking at their final destination.

The years had not been kind to the Jardine mansion. Standing about fifty feet before them, the house was supposed to have been built in the late 1700s, but the terrible condition it was in made it look even older than that. The outside walls were streaked with shiny strips of mold. The boarding all around the foundation had completely dissolved, and there was no difference in color between the gray dirt and the rotting boards of the structure. It was as if the house had risen from the dark earth itself—just sprouting one day like an evil plant.

"There they are," Sam announced, indicating several carved statues of creatures that glared down at them from the roof. "Those are gargoyles and I want one."

"And how do you suppose you're going to get one?" Louis asked, already knowing the answer.

"I figure we'll just find a way to climb up there and take one," Sam said nonchalantly. "All I have to do is decide which one I want. Come on, let's get a closer look."

The three friends made their way over the barren meadow that led to the menacing structure, and they soon found themselves only a few feet from the front door, looking up at the hideous beasts. Each statue was about the size of a small person, with features that were a cross between a lion and a dog. All had powerful-looking limbs that ended in sharp claws. They appeared to be made of marble, but with all the weather damage and the thick mold that had grown on them, the creatures now looked like they were made of grayish-green stone.

"They sure are ugly," Wally said, still breathing heavily from the bike ride. "Are you sure you could sleep with one of those in your bedroom?"

Sam smiled wickedly. "I'll probably sleep *better*."

Louis stared at the statues. "Looks like they might be heavy," he said. "How are you going to get one down?"

"I have connections," Sam said slyly, referring to his father's moving and storage business. That meant Sam had access to block-and-tackles, ropes, pulleys, and lots of other equipment he could use to lift down the gargoyle. "The only other item I might need is your little brother's wagon, Louis," Sam said. "That way we can pull my new pet home."

Louis nodded. "No problem," he said.

But Wally looked troubled as he stared up at the gargoyle nearest to them. Just looking at the thing gave him goose bumps. "I don't know," he said hesitantly. "We could get in trouble for stealing one of those things."

Sam looked astonished. "Take a good look, Wally," he gestured at the decrepit house. "No one owns this dump, no one's gonna miss one of those gargoyles. Right?"

Wally nodded uncertainly and Sam turned back to the house. "I think I like that one—on the right-hand corner," he declared, staring at his chosen gargoyle. "We'll come back tomorrow after dark and nab it."

On their way back over the bumps and twists of the dirt road, the boys were silent, each occupied with his own thoughts. Sam was trying to decide where to place his new gargoyle. Louis was getting worried that his parents would be upset because he wasn't home yet. And Wally—he just couldn't get the gargoyle's ferocious snarling mouth out of his mind. He knew it was just a statue, but to him the thing had looked, well, hungry.

As they rode down the alley behind the movie theater, Sam brought his bike to a screeching halt by the trash bins. Wally and Louis quickly braked as well.

"What are we stopping for?" Louis asked.

"A couple of weeks ago I saw ushers throwing out some old movie posters," Sam explained, "and last week *Son of Dracula* was playing. Let's see if we can find a creepy poster for my horror collection."

Wally grimaced. "I don't want to dig through trash."

But Sam just ignored both his friends. "Last one in is a six-month-old corpse," he taunted, jumping off his bike and hoisting himself up and over the rim of the huge trash bin. Shrugging, Louis followed, and finally Wally gave in as well.

As they sifted through the layers of stale popcorn, crinkled movie film, and wadded paper towels, Sam had to smile. He never had any doubt that he could get Louis and Wally to do exactly what he wanted. He was their leader and that's all there was to it.

The boys dug around in the smelly trash container for almost fifteen minutes before Sam held up a scrap of paper. "Well, I found a poster—or at least a piece of one.

"Too bad, Sam," Louis said, glancing nervously again at his watch. "Can we go home now?"

"Yeah, sure," Sam agreed. "But tomorrow we meet at my place at five o'clock sharp," he said, as they mounted their bikes. "Remember, my gargoyle's waiting for me!"

The boys rode off to their separate homes, shaking popcorn out of their clothes all the way.

Wally was one of six kids, so when he let himself in the kitchen door well after dark, no one even noticed. The family was already at the dinner table and he merely sat down and joined in. They were having pork chops, his favorite, but for some reason he'd lost his appetite. All he could think about as everyone munched away was the gargoyles ripping meat apart in some hideous feast. And, when Pogo, the family mutt, went rooting under the table for scraps and accidentally licked Wally's ankle, the boy nearly jumped right out of his skin, immediately picturing a snarling gargoyle giving him a taste.

That's when Wally excused himself and headed for his room. He plucked the dictionary off his shelf and thumbed through the "G's" until he found it.

"Gargoyle," he read aloud, his entire mouth dry just from saying the word. "A grotesque figure believed to protect the building on which it rests."

Wally slowly closed the book. Maybe he'd gotten such a bad feeling from the gargoyles at the Jardine mansion because they were protecting a place that was haunted. *We can't steal one of the gargoyles,* his mind raced. *Whatever they're protecting might get angry!*

Exhausted from the ride out to the mansion and from just plain worrying about those stupid gargoyles, Wally decided to go to bed early. And the moment his head hit the pillow, he immediately went deep into a dream.

He, Sam, and Louis were walking quietly on the roof of the Jardine mansion, slowly approaching the gargoyle Sam had picked out. Wally began to help Sam tie a rope around the creature, shuddering at how chilly its green marble skin felt to the touch. Suddenly the gargoyle came to life with a hideous roar and the rope snapped. The monster reared up from its pedestal on powerful hind legs and slashed at them with razor-sharp claws.

"Help!" Wally screamed, waking up with a start.

"Wally, are you all right?" his mother called.

His heart pounding, Wally told his mother that he'd just had a bad dream. Then he lay there in the dark for a few minutes trying to think of excuses to tell Sam for not helping him steal a gargoyle tomorrow.

Earlier that same evening after he had left his friends behind the movie theater, Sam had ridden his bike home to a dark house. His dad was out of town on business, and his mom must have already started her night shift as a nurse at the county hospital. Sometimes Sam didn't see either parent for three days straight.

Being an only child, Sam might have been lonely—*if* he'd been a different kind of boy. As it was he just let himself in and walked calmly through the house to his room, flicking on lights as he went.

When he came to his bedroom, he stood at the door for a moment and admired what he liked to call his "horror museum." Yes, the gargoyle was going to fit in beautifully. He scanned the room looking for the perfect spot for it, and then his eyes fell on the space occupied by a large trunk filled with extra bedding. If he put it there, he'd be able to see the gargoyle from both his bed and his desk, and it would be the first thing someone would lay eyes on when they entered the room.

Yes, anyone coming in here will have a good scare, Sam thought. Then wearing a satisfied smile, he headed to the kitchen to make himself dinner.

Louis didn't have much of an opinion one way or the other about the gargoyles. The Jardine mansion kind of made him uneasy, but the gargoyles didn't scare him. In fact, he was just happy to be involved in the whole adventure of nabbing one for Sam.

But his mother put an end to that.

Louis had just turned his bike down his street when he spotted her, tapping her foot beneath a streetlight in front of their house.

"Do you have any idea what time it is?" she called.

"Sorry," he said as he drew closer. "I kind of lost track of the time."

"Well, you'd better learn to keep track of it," she said. "Until then you're grounded for one more week."

"But I have plans for tomorrow," Louis begged.

"One week!" his mother repeated. "And maybe you'll think twice about missing dinner next time and worrying your father and I half to death."

"Yes Ma'am," Louis said miserably. Sam was not going to understand this at all.

The next day, the three friends sat at the school lunch tables before plates of cafeteria macaroni. "We're all set for after school, right?" Sam said between bites.

"I guess," Wally said uncertainly.

Louis couldn't meet Sam's eyes. Instead he looked down at the untouched peach cobbler as if it had suddenly become fascinating. "I can't go," he said in a tiny voice.

"What did you say?" Sam couldn't believe one of his friends would dare let him down.

"I'm sorry, Sam," Louis mumbled. "I got grounded for being late. You can still borrow the wagon though."

Wally looked hopefully at Sam, praying he'd call the whole thing off. But Sam just said, "Fine, Wally will get the wagon on his way over to my house."

And so, against his better judgment, Wally found himself walking up Sam's front walk at five o'clock sharp, towing a red wagon, with one very squeaky, very annoying back wheel.

Sam was waiting for him on the porch. "I've got everything we'll need," he said. "Bring the wagon around back and we'll load it up."

In the garage, the boys loaded the wagon with a small winch and pulley. "I tested this on a small boulder in the back yard," Sam explained. "It should pull the gargoyle right off its base and pivot it so that we can lower it to the ground."

Wally just shrugged. He didn't know much about such things, but he was sure it would work if Sam said so.

"Come on," Sam said, grabbing a flashlight. "It'll take a lot longer to get there without our bicycles."

It was already 6:30 by the time they entered the woods, and the sun had completely dropped out of the sky. Flicking on the flashlight, Sam led the way through the dark woods. Wally, his ever-dutiful servant, followed behind pulling the wagon. He was still very nervous about the whole thing, and now, being in the spooky forest, his nerves were really on edge. Trying to take his mind off his fears, Wally decided to concentrate on the small birds he kept seeing flying overhead. And then he made the mistake of asking Sam what kind they were.

"They're bats, stupid," Sam said with a sneer.

Wally stared at his friend. "B-bats?" he stuttered.

"Yeah, b-bats," Sam mocked. "You're not sc-scared, are you? Because if you are, you can—"

But just then the Jardine mansion came into view and stopped Sam's words right in his throat. It stretched to the clouds, cool and evil like a castle of black ice.

He looked at Wally whose eyes were just about to bug right out of his head. "Isn't it great?" he asked, an excited smile creeping onto his face.

Wally frowned, trying to think of a way to explain to Sam the danger that he felt they were about to put themselves in. He took a deep breath. "Uh, Sam," he began. "I think you were wrong about the gargoyles not belonging to anyone."

"What do you mean by that?" Sam asked, his fingers absentmindedly touching the curved scar on his cheek.

Wally glanced at the black mansion. "I think the gargoyles belong to the house *itself*," he said. "I think they're protecting the spirits that live inside."

Sam stared at his friend for a second, then he shook his head and chuckled. "Boy, Wally. You've even got a better imagination than me. Come on, let's go up there and get my prize."

Not knowing what else to do, Wally pulled the wagon behind his friend until they stood right before the house. He had tried to warn him. Now he'd just have to hope that Sam knew what he was doing, for both their sakes.

Sam studied the side of the house. "We can make it up this way," he said, pointing. "And see, there's my beastly friend right above us, just waiting for—"

Suddenly a bolt of lightning shot across the sky.

"Uh, oh," Sam said. "We'd better hurry. Looks like a storm's moving in." He grabbed a window frame and pulled himself onto the ledge. "Hand me the equipment, then follow me."

Wally, as always, did as Sam told him, even though, as they climbed, pieces of wood broke off in his hands and several times he thought he might fall. All around them, bits of old dried paint swirled like dandruff, and Wally couldn't seem to shake the feeling that he was crawling up a living thing. The windows seemed to bulge out at him like eyes, and the wooden surface of the mansion felt like the skin of a reptile. He was hating every second of being there, but from the looks of Sam's face, his friend was having the time of his life.

Finally, both boys had made it onto the roof, and Sam had adjusted the rope in the pulley when the first raindrops began to fall. Wally looked up. The patchy clouds had joined together like pieces of a huge, black jigsaw puzzle, and within seconds it had begun pouring.

"Wow, that came on out of nowhere!" Sam yelled into the rising wind. "Come on! Let's hurry!"

It was the moment Wally had dreaded. He peered through the splattering rain at Sam's chosen gargoyle. "Are you sure about this?" he called.

But for some reason, Sam had stopped dead and was looking up at the clouds. Instinctively, Wally looked up, too, and it seemed to take every ounce of strength he had just to turn his head. In fact, there was something odd about the raindrops as they hit his face now. They felt unusually heavy, almost as though they were made of lead . . . or marble!

Marble! That's what my legs feel like! Wally's mind screamed. And then in horror he noticed his entire body was stiffening as if gravel was being poured through his veins. He stood, unable to take another step, as shingles from the ancient roof rose up and wrapped themselves around his feet.

What's happening to me? he cried inwardly, wanting to scream, but unable to get his mouth open. *Is it happening to Sam, too?* He tried with all his might to turn his head even an inch, but he couldn't look over at his friend, and he couldn't look away from the heavy, blinding rain.

Louis didn't see either Wally or Sam for days. He called both of their homes, but their parents seemed upset and wouldn't talk to him. Finally his week's grounding was over, and as soon as school was out, he jumped on his bike and headed directly for the one place he knew they had been.

As Louis drew near the mansion, he noticed something looked different. At first he couldn't put his finger on it. He didn't see his friends anywhere. Louis walked over to his brother's wagon, standing there by the sagging front porch. He thought it was weird that the wagon was filled with water. After all, it hadn't rained in months.

Then looking up, Louis froze. There were definitely two more gargoyles on the roof, each colored a ghastly gray-green. As he stared at the two new ones, he thought he might be sick. Instead, he just started screaming, and he kept on screaming all the way home. He'd never get the images of the new gargoyles out of his head. One was slightly overweight and had a terrified look on its face, while the other held a clawed hand up to a curved scar on its cheek.

THE WARDEN'S FISHPOND – 1967

One warm Sunday in April, a bunch of friends and I wandered up to the Jardine mansion. The old place has a field in front of it where nothing grows that serves as a perfect baseball diamond.

We were having a pretty good game that afternoon. It was all tied up at six to six when I stepped up to the plate, facing Shorty Roberts, the best pitcher in town.

"You'll never hit this one, Cory!" he called to me.

Well, that made me mad, so when he pitched it, I put everything I had into my swing and I surprised everyone —especially myself—by hitting a home run. The only problem was, the ball landed over by the mansion.

"Way to go, Cory!" Mikie Sellars yelled when I came around to touch home base. Mikie is one of the little second graders who always comes up to watch us play. "Can I get the ball for you guys?" he asked.

I looked back. I'd whacked that ball so far that getting me out would've been impossible. No one had even thought of chasing after it yet. "Yeah. Thanks, Mikie," I said. Not thinking he'd have any trouble, I watched him running off, still holding his can of soda.

Both teams stood there waiting, talking, and tossing stones into the forest. And then we noticed that Mikie was gone a long time. A few of us speculated that he might've gotten himself lost in the woods, and we were about to go after him when he finally came running back—*without* the ball.

Poor little kid, he was crying so hard he couldn't talk. Then finally he managed to show us the sleeve of his sweatshirt. It was all torn and shredded.

"Something must have attacked him," Shorty guessed. He looked toward the mansion, fear turning his face a chalky white. "Something with sharp teeth. Was it a bear, Mikie? Or a mountain lion?"

"Maybe it was a raccoon. Coons can be vicious if you get near their holes," Eddie Lamb suggested.

But Mikie shook his head. "No," he finally managed to say between sobs. "It was a *fish!*"

Now, the thing I like most in the whole world is fishing. I've done it since I was seven years old when my stepdad, Tom, started taking me. That's why I knew for sure that there wasn't anything bigger than a goldfish within miles of this town. You see, Tom and I had to drive into the next county to even find a river or lake to fish in, and the only thing a fish ever attacked was our bait. Still, the more I looked at the expression in Mikie's tear-filled eyes, the more I got to thinking that maybe, somehow, a fish really *had* come after him.

"Come on," I said to my friends. "Let's go take a look."

"No way," Eddie said. "I'm not going near that house."

In fact, everyone else shook their heads or looked down at their feet. I just stared at them. There was a rumor that the Jardine mansion was haunted, but I didn't know that any of my friends actually *believed* it was true.

"Suit yourselves," I said. "I guess I'll just go by myself."

As I walked over, the cold shadow of the mansion fell on me. I looked up at the house, at its black, decayed face, and I could see how the other kids let their imagination get the best of them. I looked back for a second, and saw everyone watching me, fear in their eyes.

"What a bunch of babies," I muttered under my breath. Turning back toward the mansion, I suddenly heard a loud splash coming from around the side, so I hurried over.

There, before my surprised eyes, was a huge fishpond. I'd heard a lot about the Jardine place, but I never heard about this. Starting to actually believe Mikie, I cautiously walked over to the pond, stood at the edge, and strained to see the bottom through all the algae and water plants. Could a fish actually be living in that murky water? And had it really attacked little Mikie Sellars?

I looked around and saw his soda can by the edge of the pond, so I knew he'd been here, all right. But I didn't see any sign of a fish, or our baseball. So I ran back to the field and reported to the group what I'd seen.

After an uncomfortable silence, Eddie cleared his throat. "The ball must've sunk to the bottom," he said, his eyes darting toward the house. "Guess the game's over."

We all began strolling home, and as we walked, I had only one thing on my mind. I wanted to get home and bring my fishing gear back to that strange pond.

And within an hour, there I was, standing by the pond's edge, the sun hanging low in the sky and a chill wind starting to whistle through the trees in the forest.

I looked at the green water before me. Flies and mosquitoes were skittering across the surface. If this had been a normal pond, fish would have been swimming hungrily toward them, making it a perfect time for a good catch. But since I had no idea what kind of fish might be lurking in this foul-smelling water, I had trouble deciding what kind of bait to use.

I ended up trying nearly every lure, spinner, and salmon egg in my tackle box. Again and again I cast my line into the pond, but nothing struck my hooks except a weird old kid's ball with a clown's face drawn on it.

As I sat there, waiting for a bite, the sun slowly sank into the forest. Bored, I studied the mansion, which stood only about fifteen feet away. It really was a creepy place, I decided. The wood covering the exterior was dark as tar, and something about the odd reflections in its ancient, unwashed windowpanes made me kind of nervous, as if something might be watching me from within.

Shuddering, I decided I would try one last time with something new—an earthworm I'd spotted wriggling in the moist earth near the waterline of the pond.

I was threading the squirming creature on the hook when I suddenly felt a sharp pain race through my thumb. "Ouch!" I cried, seeing that I'd cut myself on the barbed end of the hook. Immediately, blood oozed out, covering the worm, and splattering all over my pants.

"This is not turning out to be one of my better fishing afternoons," I muttered to no one as I wrapped a rag around my thumb. I almost packed up and left, right then and there, but I'd promised myself one last try, so I whipped back my pole and made a final cast.

To my amazement, there was an instant splashing, and then my rod bent nearly in two! I'd certainly hooked onto something—and it was *big*.

For a while it was all I could do just to hold onto my pole, and then the fish and I began to fight each other. Now, in my five years of fishing I have battled bonita, marlin, and tuna. Once I even caught a sailfish when Tom took us for a vacation in the Gulf of Mexico. But never once had I ever had a fight like the one with the thing from that pond.

Astonished, I watched my line whipping all over the place. It was like I'd hooked a big old dog that was straining on the end of a leash. Then, all at once, the creature appeared to be resting. It lay so motionless that I thought I might have lost it . . . until suddenly the line spun out so quickly that the reel hummed like a bee. It was incredibly strange—not at all the kind of fight you would expect in an oversized fishpond. No, this thing on the end of my line was fighting as if it had the entire ocean as its battlefield.

Finally, I wore it down. I worked until the line was only a few feet long, then I swung the fish out of the water and into my net. For a moment, I just sat there, trying to catch my breath, as it thrashed around. Then I decided to have a good look at my catch.

Since I had no flashlight, I leaned toward the fish and squinted at it in the moonlight. It had several rows of sharp fins and a head that seemed unusually large for its body. I felt a small tingle of fear along my spine as I remembered that this fish, whatever it was, hadn't wanted my lures or salmon eggs. It hadn't been interested in anything at all—until it got a taste of that earthworm . . . with my blood on it.

Shuddering, I decided that I'd had enough of this place. I quickly dumped the net into a big bag I'd brought with me, grabbed my tackle box and pole, and left.

On my way home I passed by Dr. McGee's and I decided to stop in. He was the town taxidermist, and he worked right out of his own home. In fact, he'd stuffed and mounted most everything my stepdad and I caught.

"Cory!" he said, a big smile lifting the ends of his mustache when he saw me on his doorstep. "What brings you here at this late hour?"

I handed him the sack. "I've got a job for you," I replied. "But be careful, I don't even know what this one *is*."

Dr. McGee's smile never wavered. "I've had some experience with this, you know." He chuckled. "Fact is, I've never had a fish get the better of me yet."

I left the sack, waved, and stepped out the door. But as I headed home, I couldn't help but hope that Dr. McGee hadn't met his match.

The next day I stopped in at Dr. McGee's house after school. It seemed like I had to knock a long time before I finally heard his footsteps on the hardwood floor inside. When he opened the door, his face was like stone.

"Where did you catch this thing, Cory?" he asked.

"It was in a big pond, up near that old mansion in the woods," I told him. "What kind of fish is it, anyway?"

"It's all mounted. Come see," he replied mysteriously.

I followed him into his study, and there on his desk, attached to a long oval of mahogany wood, was a monster. It was close to three feet long with several rows of spiny fins covering its body. The head, though, was the real showstopper. It was a huge ebony ball with *three*, small hooded eyes, and a mouth crammed with the sharpest, most wicked-looking teeth I'd ever seen.

"You'd better stay away from that pond," Dr. McGee said. "With those teeth, this thing might be some mutated relative of piranha—and as you know, a school of piranha can strip a cow to its bones in minutes."

I nodded, feeling as if I were in a daze. I had never seen anything as terrible as that fish.

Dr. McGee held the door for me as I struggled with the thing, which must have weighed a good thirty-five pounds. "Cory?" he said, as I stepped out onto the porch. "Be careful how you hold it. Those teeth are incredibly sharp." Then he held up his hands for me to see. They were covered with bandages.

My mom made a face when she saw what I'd brought into the house. For a while, all she could do was stare at it, then she told me that I better not even think I was going to put it up anywhere in our home.

I was a little surprised. She had never kept me and Tom from decorating the walls with our catches, no matter how ugly the fish was. "How about if I put it up in my room where you won't have to look at it?" I asked.

She shrugged. "I suppose that's all right."

And so I headed up the stairs, wondering if I actually wanted that thing in my room.

"What kind of a fish is that?" my mom called after me.

"I have no idea," I answered. "Dr. McGee didn't know, so I'm hoping Tom can identify it." Tom was the most amazing fisherman I'd ever seen. If anyone could figure out what this monstrosity was, he could. But he was away on a fly-fishing trip, so I'd have to wait until tomorrow.

In the meantime, I mounted the thing in a far corner of my room and forgot about it. But later, as I lay in bed, I couldn't help looking over at my bizarre prize. Although it was dark, the fangs of the fish seemed to glow in a beam of moonlight stealing through the blinds. It made the fish look like it was smiling at me.

But even more frightening was the soft thumping I started to hear coming from the direction of the mounted fish. At first I thought it was just my imagination running wild, or maybe just the beating of my own heart. But then the sound grew louder and more regular. In a panic I flicked on the lamp on my nightstand.

But oddly enough, as soon as the light went on the noise stopped. Nothing seemed wrong when I stared, wide-eyed, around my room—not even when I glanced over at the fish, laying motionless on its oval of wood, just like the stuffed thing should do. Still, as soon as I turned off the light again, the noise came back.

I told myself that what I was thinking wasn't possible. I tried pressing my pillow over my ears, but still I heard the thumping, all through the night. It was a soft drumming sound—exactly like a fishtail hitting the wall.

I woke exhausted the next morning. In spite of all my logic, by now I was so scared of that creepy old fish I wouldn't even look at it. I dressed quickly and left for school, bent on finding out exactly what it was that I'd caught during my lunch break.

The town had lived with the Jardine mansion since it was built in 1798, so I figured the school library would have some information on it. Sure enough, I found something on the house in a volume about the county's early history, but there was no information on what kind of fish the pond had been stocked with. All I learned was the same old stuff I'd heard in rumors, that the house was said to be haunted by three prisoners who were hired to build the place—pond and all.

I sat in the school library, gazing off in thought. I'd read that the prisoners, who were chained in the basement, had drowned during a huge storm that flooded the place. What if the pond, which was on a lower level than the house, was filled by the runoff during that terrible storm that killed the convicts? What if their angry spirits somehow got inside the fish I caught?

I slammed the dusty old volume shut. In all my life, I had never believed in ghostly things and I wasn't about to start now. There had to be some other explanation. Maybe I had simply caught a deformed fish. And maybe the thumping I had heard the night before was just a rat in the walls. Still, for the rest of the day, my thoughts were consumed with that horrible fish.

Tom finally got home from his fishing trip at about nine o'clock that night. I was writing out my Social Studies homework, trying to keep from glancing at the plaque in the corner, when he poked his head in my room.

"When school's out you'll have to come with me to the river I just fished," he said. It had some beautiful—" He stopped mid-sentence, walked into the room, and stood before the plaque. Then he gave a low whistle and shook his head. "Where'd you get this?" he asked, his eyes scanning the fish's teeth, now gleaming like needles.

"I caught it in the pond by the Jardine mansion," I answered, afraid I might get in trouble for even going near the place. "I was hoping you could tell me what it is?"

Tom was silent for a long time. Finally he turned and looked me in the eye. "I've never seen anything like it," he said flatly. Then seeing my dejected expression, he quickly added, "But I can sure get ahold of some people that will know. I'll make some phone calls right after I've taken some measurements. Do you still have that tape measure in your tackle box?"

I nodded, but right then I had a feeling that no one in the world would know what kind of fish this was.

As I watched while Tom extended the tape I'd given him from the tip of the fish's monstrous head to the end of its tail, I suddenly felt like I'd better warn him to be careful like Dr. McGee had told me. But before I had a chance to open my mouth, the creature's black brow wrinkled, and all three of the eyes scowled. Then it reared its head off the plaque and sunk its teeth right into Tom's wrist.

We both screamed at the same time, as the tape measure flew to the carpet, and Tom wrenched his arm away. "What in the world?" he sputtered, looking totally confused as he held his wound trying to keep the blood from dribbling down his arm.

My mom was there in seconds. "What happened?" she cried, seeing Tom, holding his arm and bleeding all over the place.

"The fish bit him!" I blurted out, nearly in tears.

"Don't be silly," Tom said, his voice hoarse as he let my mom help him into the bathroom where she washed and bandaged the wound. "It was my own clumsiness. I was trying to measure the darned thing and I cut myself on its teeth."

"Well, I'm taking you to the emergency room," my mom said, her face alarmed as blood seeped right through the bandage. Then she turned to me. "Cory, I want you to stay away from that thing. Do you hear me?"

I nodded dumbly, then in a flash, they were gone.

For awhile I just stared at that horrible fish with Tom's blood still dripping from its fangs. I knew what I'd seen, and I knew what had to be done. The only way to make everything right would be to return the monster to the pond. Resolved, I carefully slipped the plaque off the wall and into the same sack I'd used to carry the fish off in the first place. Then I gathered the sack, a flashlight, and my fishing knife and left the house.

When I saw the mansion this time, my feelings about it were entirely different than they had been this morning. The windows, cold in the blackness, seemed to waver with the same strange reflections I'd noticed earlier, but this time I knew it wasn't my imagination. There *was* something very wrong here, and I had the proof in my sack.

I knelt before the dark waters of the pond, then carefully I slipped the sack away, and the plaque thumped to the ground. Now the only problem was freeing the creature from the oval base. I was afraid to get too close to it, so I held my fishing knife out at arm's length and started to pry the side of the fish away from the wood. It took a good fifteen minutes to get it loose.

"There you go," I whispered to the fish as I shoved it into the water with the plaque. "You're back home."

I started to walk away, but my curiosity drew me back to the pond's edge. Unable to stop myself, I shined the beam of my flashlight into the dark water, and was fascinated to see that the stuffed fish was alive again.

And then my flashlight beam fell on something that made my mouth fall open. The fish had been more dangerous than I had thought. For there in the green and brown muck at the bottom of the pond was our baseball . . . sitting on a heap of human bones.

ONE OF THE GANG — 1988

Jeremy stood on the porch of the old mansion, waiting. He was supposed to meet somebody here tonight— that much he was sure of—but who? Frowning as he stared at the gnarled pine trees in the starlight, he tried to remember. His forgetfulness was starting to scare him, and he was beginning to think he was going crazy.

Pacing back and forth across the creaking porch boards, he tried to recall who was going to meet him. Hopefully that person would remind him why they had decided to meet here of all places—at a house that was supposed to be haunted.

Finally a tall boy with a crew cut swaggered up the walk, followed by a small band of kids. He pointed at the mansion. "There's our treasure chest," he announced.

"How we gonna get in, Winston?" asked a small boy with bright red hair.

"Just leave that to me, Red," the kid with the crew cut said.

Jeremy didn't recognize any of these people, but it was clear that Winston was the leader. When they climbed the stairs to the porch, Jeremy stepped from the shadows.

"Hi," he said, shyly. But no one acknowledged him, so Jeremy decided to just fall in with the pack.

Two in the group were girls. They, like the five boys and Winston, wore odd-looking clothes that Jeremy had never seen before. Their shirts and pants were all different colors and Jeremy felt like he stood out in his boring white shirt and black pants. In fact, one of the kids was staring right at him, and Jeremy, feeling self-conscious, turned away, afraid to meet his gaze. They were all pretty tough-looking, and seemed to care less that Jeremy was there.

The red-haired kid brushed passed Jeremy, went right up to the front door, and rattled the knob. "It's locked," he reported. "Now what, Winston?"

"Stand back," Winston ordered, stepping up to the door. "I'll take care of it." Then he threw back his leg and kicked with all his might. Instantly, the doorknob plate ripped from the old wood and clattered to the porch. Everyone cheered as the door slowly creaked open.

Jeremy gulped. Winston had broken into the mansion! Were they here to vandalize the place? His first reaction was to slip back into the shadows and run away. But then he started thinking. He had been waiting to meet these kids, hadn't he? That meant he must be a part of their group. As far as he could recall, he'd never vandalized anything in his life, so this group probably wasn't here to do that either. But what *were* they here for? Deciding that the only way to find out, Jeremy followed the kids inside.

Once inside, several of the kids lit candles, then they all gathered around Winston.

"All right, everyone," he said, his voice echoing between the rotten walls laced here and there with gigantic cobwebs. "What are we all looking for?"

"Anything we can sell!" the group yelled back.

Winston grinned. "This place has been abandoned for almost two hundred years," he went on, "so any old furniture, clothes, or other junk we can find is probably worth something. As you know, my uncle owns an antique shop, and he'll pay us cash for anything we find, no questions asked. Of course, I'll take a small fee for finding this place, then we'll split the rest. Any questions?"

"What about ghosts?" one of the boys asked quietly.

Winston chuckled. "You *believe* in that stuff, Ralph."

The other kids took Winston's lead and laughed, as Ralph's face turned bright red. "It's possible, Winston, and you know it," he said defensively. "A lot of people have died or disappeared here."

"I do feel kind of a, well, *presence* here," a girl called Missy admitted. "Hasn't anyone else felt it?"

Nobody else said a word, but Jeremy noticed that the other kids were quiet now, all looking nervously to Winston for an answer. Their leader scowled at each of them in turn. "Anyone who's scared can leave right now!" he barked.

If Jeremy had not been so shy, he would have come to Ralph's defense, too. He *did* believe in ghosts, and he thought this spooky house would probably be the perfect spot for them. Still, he didn't dare leave and risk being ridiculed by all the others.

"All right, then," Winston said, seeing that he'd over-powered everyone once again. "We want to search this entire place. When you find something, bring it back here and I'll decide if it's worth taking. Got it?"

"Where do we look?" Red asked.

"Everywhere," Winston answered. He then grabbed a picture off the wall, holding it high for everyone to see. The portrait had yellowed with time, but the image of a girl wearing a hair-ribbon could still be made out. "Here's an example of what I mean," he said. "Even if this painting isn't worth anything, the frame might be." He set it on the floor near the door. "Okay, scram!"

The kids scattered, each of them choosing a different direction, and Jeremy didn't know where to go. He didn't like the idea of stealing things, but he knew he had to stick with this group until he could figure out how he fit in here. He noticed that Ralph and Missy had teamed up and had headed off down the hall. Since he thought Ralph was probably the most sensible kid in the group, Jeremy decided to hang around with them. He sure didn't like the idea of running into a ghost on his own.

As the three of them headed up the stairs, Jeremy saw that there were discolored places where more pictures had hung on the walls, and he figured that other people had already grabbed them. As they reached the top, Missy cleared her throat. "I think you were brave to stand up to Winston," she said admiringly. "I think it's very possible this place could be haunted."

"Me too," Jeremy agreed, wanting desperately to fit in.

Ralph gazed over the side of the railing at the kids milling around below. "All my life I've gotten this strange feeling inside when something spooky is about to happen," he said. "I've got that feeling right now."

Jeremy looked about, his eyes wide with fear, wondering what it was that Ralph sensed. He certainly had had an uneasy feeling ever since he'd arrived at this house.

"Well, let's get this over with and get out of here," Missy said. She pushed at the first door in the hall, and they all peeked inside and saw a rotting bed in the center of the room. Ancient reddish stains dotted the floor.

I know this room, Jeremy thought, suddenly struck with the feeling that someone he knew had done something in here, although Jeremy wasn't sure what.

As Jeremy looked about the room, trying to recall why the place was so familiar to him, Missy took down an old cracked wall mirror and Ralph carried out a small end table. Empty-handed, Jeremy followed them downstairs where the pair laid the furniture on a growing pile of loot by the door. Winston was there, checking everything as it was carried over. "Nice table," he mumbled to Ralph. But he shook his head at Missy's mirror. "Too bad the glass is broken," he said. "Leave it here. The frame's all rotting, too." He looked right at Jeremy. "What do you have, kid?"

Jeremy was just about to say, "Nothing," when someone behind him said, "Just this."

Whipping around, Jeremy saw a curly-haired boy holding up an old rag doll. Then Jeremy heard Ralph calling Missy from another room, so he headed off with her.

"I found a door that I think goes down to a basement," Ralph said. "Want to take a look?"

"Why not?" Jeremy replied.

"Sure," Missy said. "Let me light another candle."

Sure enough, behind the door was a series of stone steps, covered with slippery moss. It was very dark, and as they neared the bottom, Jeremy was again struck with the same odd sensation he'd had upstairs. Something had happened here to someone he knew.

"You know that feeling I told you about knowing when something spooky is about to happen?" Ralph asked as he stood in the middle of the room, holding a candle. "Well, I think I'm having one right now."

Jeremy shuddered. The candlelight created scary shadows on the mold-covered walls. Then suddenly a glint of something metal pierced the darkness. Jeremy went over for a closer look, and found a chain sticking out of the rock wall. For some reason, the sight stirred something deep inside Jeremy, and all at once he felt he was on the verge of remembering everything. "Bring your candles over here!" he called urgently.

But neither Missy nor Ralph answered him. In fact, although Missy was looking right at him she said, "Come on, Ralph. I don't see anything worth taking down here."

"Yeah, let's get out of here," Ralph replied.

Jeremy felt a sudden pang of anger. Why were they totally ignoring him? This time he shouted, "Hey! Don't either of you hear me?" But his only answer was the cat-squeak of the door as it shut above him.

Stunned, Jeremy stood there in the middle of the pitch-black basement, and then, growing panicked, he flew up the steps after them. He was usually a quiet, shy kid, but when he was angry, all of that changed. He walked right up to Ralph and Missy and shouted at them, "Hey! Why did you leave me down there in the dark?"

Neither of them said a word. *What am I doing wrong?* Jeremy wondered. Dejected, he kicked at an old piece of tin lying on the floor and sent it flying across the room.

"Did you see that?" Missy said, looking very pale.

"I sure did," Ralph replied, walking over and holding his light up to the scrap of metal. He was only a foot or so from Jeremy, but he never even glanced at him. "It looks like a piece of an old suit of armor."

Suddenly Winston strode up. "What's all the noise over here?" he asked. "Are you two imagining things again?"

"This armor just flew across the room," Ralph said.

"Yeah—so what?" Winston snapped. "Maybe a rat got inside it or something!"

"Oh *sure*," Missy said sarcastically. "Come on, Ralph. Let's get out of here."

Ralph and Missy started to walk toward the door. Then all of a sudden Ralph turned around. "Listen, Winston," he said. "I know you don't believe in spirits, but there's something in this house. I think everybody should leave."

"We have a job to do here!" Winston spat.

Ralph and Missy hustled through the broken door. Gathering all his courage, Jeremy stepped out of the shadows right in front of Winston.

"Winston," he said, a small tremor in his voice. "Can you see me?"

But Winston simply turned and walked away.

For several minutes, Jeremy couldn't move as the realization hit him. If no one could see him and no one could hear him, that only meant that . . . he was a *ghost!*

Lost in confusing thoughts, wondering when he had died, Jeremy now understood that Winston and his gang were not the ones he was supposed to meet at the mansion. But who *was* he supposed to meet here.

Following a strange urge inside him, Jeremy wandered into the backyard. He passed an old fishpond and headed around an ancient trellis that had fallen from the house years ago. Soon he'd reached the edge of the property line, where the forest sprang up before him. It was as if he'd been drawn to this spot, and now Jeremy looked about, wondering if he might find some answers here.

The tips of what appeared to be three small trees poked out near his feet. Jeremy frowned, trying to figure out how saplings could grow here when the rest of the yard was so barren. He leaned down and brushed earth aside from one of the small trees, and quickly saw that it wasn't a tree at all. It was a marker . . . for a grave!

He quickly uncovered the other two markers, then stepped back and stood at the foot of three graves. Then all at once, Jeremy felt a strange chill bearing down on him. A foggy mist was coming out of the center grave! It quickly assembled itself into the shape of a man. Wearing the striped uniform of a convict, the man broke into a twisted smile. "Well, my boy," the ghostly figure said in a hollow voice. "You're right on time!"

Jeremy suddenly recognized who it was before him. "Father?" he mumbled. "What's going on here?"

His father's reddish eyes flicked toward the mansion. Lights flickered in the windows. "Ah, we have company," he said. A hungry expression came over him. "It would be rude to keep them waiting, so I'll try to explain things quickly." He put a ghostly hand on Jeremy's shoulder. "You and I only meet here once a year, son," he began. "That's probably why you're having trouble remembering. We used to meet here all the time, but now there are many spirits with whom we must share this house."

"What's so special about tonight?" Jeremy asked.

The ghost smiled warmly. "This is the anniversary of my death," he explained. "I was killed in this house nearly two centuries ago. I was a prisoner within weeks of being released, and the warden had brought me and two others here to help build his new home. But alas, the warden forgot all about us during a thunderstorm, and we drowned, chained in the basement."

Jeremy remembered the chain he'd seen down there. "But why am *I* here, father?" he asked, frowning.

"You had been in an orphanage, awaiting my release," said the ghost, with a sad look. "When I died, the orphanage turned you out in the streets, where you died soon after. You see, the miserable man who killed me was responsible for your death, too. That is why once a year we both return to the mansion."

"But what do we do here, Father?" Jeremy persisted.

A deathly grin spread across the ghost's face. "Take my hand," he said, his voice deep and unearthly. "I'll show you."

"Wonderful!" Winston cried, as the last of his loot was laid at his feet. "I'd say we've made a small fortune tonight!"

"Hooray!" the group cheered, proud of their hard work.

Winston rubbed his hands together, staring greedily at the carved headboards, silver candelabras, and old china plates before him. "Now we have to get this stuff out of here. Red, would you be so good as to open the door?"

Red smiled and grabbed the doorknob. "Hey, wait a minute. Didn't you kick this door in, Winston?"

"That's right," Winston replied, a bewildered look on his face. He pushed Red away and grabbed the knob. "Hey! It's locked!"

Suddenly a great shrieking sound filled the house. At the same time, the unmistakable sound of chains rattling filtered up from the basement. And behind everything, the boom of thunder shook the entire mansion. Terrified, the kids all looked to Winston.

"D-d-don't worry!" Winston stammered. "I have everything under—" But his words caught in his throat just as all the candles burnt out at once.

Finally Jeremy knew what he was, and where he belonged, and it was certainly not with Winston and his gang. As they hovered through the air, Jeremy glanced at his father, who with his skeleton face and red eyes was about as horrible a sight as one could stand to see. And yet, Jeremy only hoped that someday he could be just like him.

"You go ahead, son," his father urged, pointing at the group of kids cowering by the front door. "Let 'em have it."

"Thanks, Father," Jeremy replied, and then with all of his might he let out a bloodcurdling howl and flew at the frightened kids.

EVIL IN THE ASHES — PRESENT DAY

It is late evening, and all is quiet as Sarah crouches in the bushes, watching.

There is nothing to see at first. Just a house, older than time, rotting in a dead meadow. No footsteps echo along its corridors. No breeze stirs in the nearby forest. But Sarah is patient. It is close to midnight, and she knows that soon, activity will strike the old mansion.

It begins with the silencing of the crickets. One minute she hears them, chirping happily, and the next, there is no sound at all. Sarah knows that some strange instinct must have quieted the insects. Still she can't help imagining that some invisible, evil force has reached from the old house and crushed the life out of them.

Shivering, Sarah checks her watch. Then she takes out her notebook and records the date and time.

A minute later the wind reaches her. It feels as cold as the breath of a glacier, and Sarah knows this unearthly wind is blowing from the mansion.

Her fingers trembling, Sarah again takes note of the time and writes it down in her notebook. She glances up, surprised to see dull greenish lights already beginning to flicker behind the windows. The mansion looks like some multi-eyed creature awakening from sleep.

This is the part she hates the most. Sarah knows it's no longer safe for her to pay attention to her note taking. She sets down her pen, flattens herself into the tall grass, and watches intently.

The lights grow brighter and greener. The outline of the house shimmers and bulges against the night sky. The entire top floor appears to be growing bigger, like a balloon with someone squeezing it at the bottom. Rays of green light shine from the structure into the forest, up into the sky . . . and toward the town.

Now the cold wind brings a howling sound to Sarah's ears. Whenever she's been here and heard this howling, it has always made her imagine strange and horrible things. Tonight, the howling is ferocious. And as it grows louder, Sarah sees that the top of the mansion has enlarged to such an extent it looks as if it might explode.

She must not stay here another second. And so, Sarah grabs her notebook and runs.

"Last night was your night, wasn't it, Sarah?" Amanda asks, chewing thoughtfully on her sandwich.

Sarah has been unusually quiet today, and the other kids can tell that something's on her mind. This is scary, because everyone knows she was the last one to take the watch at the mansion. A hush falls over the cafeteria. Several kids crowd forward near Sarah and Amanda's lunch table, listening.

Sarah shakes her head. "It's worse," she says in a small voice. Taking out her notebook, she flips through the pages, then stops at the most recent entry. "The lights appeared in the windows only about a minute after the cold wind began," she reports. "And the howling began only seconds after the house started swelling."

The other kids stare in uncomfortable silence, unable to comprehend how bad things have become. "The mansion has gotten more powerful," Amanda concludes. "Everyone in this town is in danger."

"But what are we going to do about it?" one of the kids surrounding the table asks.

Amanda shrugs. "Not much we *can* do—unless we get our parents to help us."

Sarah shakes her head. "Amanda, the Jardine mansion is haunted. Every kid in town believes that, but not one adult does."

"Then maybe it's time to tell them how we've been taking turns watching the place for the last two years," Amanda answers. She studies the faces around her, making brief eye contact with each kid. "None of the adults ever go near the Jardine mansion. We've got to get some of them out there at midnight so they can see what we've seen. Maybe we should even show them the journal we've been keeping."

Mitchell, a tall eighth-grader with wire-rim glasses, steps to the front of the group. "I'll say it's changed," he says. "Remember how at first we only saw spirits now and then? Now they're out there practically all the time."

"And thunderstorms used to stir up out of nowhere," someone comments.

"Yeah, and the sound of chains rattling," someone else adds with a shudder.

Amanda holds up the journal. "All of that's nothing compared to the way it is now," she says. "Is it, Sarah?"

"It's not even the same place," Sarah agrees. "It's as if all the ghosts that used to haunt the place have combined into a single evil presence. In fact, it's grown so powerful I don't even think it's safe for us to even *watch* the mansion any more."

Mitchell sighs, pushing his glasses higher on his nose with his thumb. "Well, my mom and dad aren't going to believe a word of any of this," he says. "But I'll tell them if you think it's a good idea, Amanda."

"I think it's our only hope," Amanda says gravely. "I'll talk to my folks, too. Tonight. I don't know if they'll buy it, but I think my grandmother will." She looks at the crowd of kids. "Who's with us?"

One by one, hands go up, and within minutes the cafeteria is filled with silent kids, all raising their hands in a show of support. Amanda nods at everyone, then notices that Sarah is the only one in the room who still has both hands lying flat on the table. "What about you, Sarah?" she demands.

But Sarah has been lost in a horrible daydream. She remembers the bulging top of the mansion, looking as if it would burst any second like an erupting volcano, showering the entire town with ghosts and ghouls and unspeakable things. Even if they could get all the adults in the world to help them, what could they possibly do against that kind of evil? But for now, with all the kids staring her way, Sarah holds back from speaking her true feelings. Slowly, she too raises her hand. "I'll try," she says, but her throat feels as dry as sand.

That night, Sarah sits across from her mother at the dinner table. A steaming casserole of microwave lasagna sits between them, a dish Sarah usually loves. But tonight she has no appetite. She wonders how many other kids in Creighton are feeling the same way as they try to broach the subject with their parents.

Her mother looks up from her food. "Are you feeling all right?" she asks, pointing at Sarah's untouched meal.

Sarah shrugs. "Actually, Mom," she says hesitantly, "there was something I needed to talk to you about."

Without speaking her mother sets down her fork and looks deep into Sarah's eyes. "Go on," she says simply.

"It's about that old house off in the hills," Sarah begins. "You know, the old Jardine mansion?"

Her mother chuckles, and her eyes grow dreamy. "I remember that place. When I was a kid, we all thought it was haunted."

"It is haunted," Sarah says quietly.

Her mom's smile fades. "What are you getting at?"

Sarah takes a deep breath. It's now or never. "Mom, a bunch of us kids have been watching that house for a long time now," she blurts out. "We've got a feeling it's a dangerous place. Late at night, there are all kinds of noises and lights that come from it and—"

"Late at night?" her mom repeats angrily. "Young lady, are you telling me you've been sneaking out joining your friends at the Jardine mansion when I've thought you're in bed?"

"Not exactly," Sarah says, feeling the heat rise in her face and hearing her voice become a whisper. "Actually, I've only been assigned to go there about once a month, and when I do, I'm always alone."

"*Assigned!* Are you and your friends playing secret agents?" her mother snaps. "Is that what this is—some kind of silly game?"

"It's not a game, Mom," Sarah protests. "It's kind of hard to describe, but we think that the Jardine mansion is, well, coming *alive.*"

Sarah's mother pushes back her chair, and begins pacing the kitchen. "I can't understand why a group of kids your age would pull something like this behind your parents' backs!"

"Because none of the adults will believe it!" Sarah yells back. "And the funny thing is, you used to believe it when you were a kid. You said so yourself!"

"But this is nonsense, Sarah," her mother says, growing more and more exasperated. "Sure I believed in ghosts as a kid, but as an adult, I realize that—"

"Okay, then why don't you come with me to the mansion tonight and see for yourself," Sarah interrupts. "We won't be alone—there should be *lots* of other parents there, too."

"Oh, really," her mother says, raising an eyebrow. Then she turns and heads toward the kitchen phone. "Let's just find out."

All across the town a chain reaction happens. At first, the parents try to laugh off what their kids are telling them. Then they grow angry, and finally they call other parents. As their children described again and again what they've witnessed at the mansion, make bargains, and plead with their parents to at least consider going with them, the adults eventually wear down. In the end, most of the town—adults and kids alike—agree to meet at the mansion in a few hours, just before midnight.

Soon a parade of flashlights is winding its way through the streets of Creighton toward the edge of the dark woods where the mansion sits. Parents walk with their children, and hardly anyone speaks to anyone. Many of the adults are grumpy for having given in to such nonsense. And all of the kids are speechless, amazed that they've finally gotten their parents to listen to them about the Jardine mansion.

As the crowd enters the forest, beams from hundreds of flashlights cast flickering shadows on the twisted trees, making them look as if they're moving. Then, as everyone approaches the crest of the hill, the trees die out, giving way to a barren meadow. All the kids know that this means they are getting close, for nothing grows near the mansion.

At the top of a slight rise, the terrible house comes into view, and the entire group stops as one and stares.

In the dry meadow beyond, it crouches—almost as if it's been waiting for them. While most of the hard dirt is lit by uneven moonlight, the mansion remains in shadow—dark, mysterious, and uninviting.

Without a word, the crowd gathers in the meadow, staying a safe distance from the menacing structure. People glance at their watches. "It's almost midnight," someone whispers.

Standing next to her mother, Sarah feels a mixture of anticipation and fear. What if nothing happens? And worse—what if something *terrible* happens? She considers the black, crumbling house before them, remembering the things she's seen here. What if the house has been waiting, storing up evil for all these years, planning to use it all at once on this very night?

Wondering if any of her friends are thinking the same things, Sarah scans the crowd, looking for anyone she knows. But it is too dark to spot anybody.

Suddenly a father's mocking voice disturbs the silence. "Well, Toby," he says, addressing his son. "It's five past midnight. Where are all these ghosts?"

Other parents start grumbling, too. "I don't know how we all got caught up in this," says some woman with a high-pitched voice.

"Did you kids get together and plan this as some kind of hoax?" an angry father asks. "Are you trying to make fools of us?"

Sarah's own mother sighs, looking down at her daughter in frustration. "Well?" she asks.

"The house must sense we're all out here," Sarah guesses. "It *always* starts glowing around midnight, but for some reason tonight it's waiting."

"Obviously the house doesn't *always* do anything," her mother replies sarcastically. "And if I find out that you're part of some joke the other kids are pulling, you're going to be grounded."

Just then a middle-aged man with long gray hair walks from the crowd. The kids only know him as "Crazy Louie," the guy who does odd jobs around town and sleeps in the public park. Right now he's pointing up at the roof of the house with a weird expression on his face. "See those gargoyles?" he says. Everyone looks up to see nine or ten mold-covered gargoyles perched on the rain gutters. "They all used to be children! I know, because when I was a kid—"

"Cool it, Louie!" someone shouts. "No one wants to hear that tired old story of yours."

As Louie wanders off, a disturbed look in his eyes, Mr. Sellars, the town grocer, steps out and addresses the crowd. He's wearing the smug expression of an adult who no longer believes in the things that scared him when he was a child. "When I was a kid, there used to be a fishpond over on the side of the mansion," he announces. "I'm going to see if it's still there."

"Check it out for us, Mikie!" yells one of his friends. "And watch out for those attack fish!"

Everyone laughs as they watch him stroll behind the mansion, sipping leisurely on a can of soda. The crowd is noisy now. Some of the adults are quite angry with their kids, threatening a variety of punishments. Others are trying to laugh it off. Sarah ignores them all, watching for the man with the soda can to return, afraid that he might not.

But soon he does return, his face a chalky white. He no longer holds the can. "There's something still alive in that fishpond!" he says hoarsely. "Something big!" His friends help him to sit down, patting him on the back as if he were a little kid. "Sure, Mikie," they say. "Sure."

A young man with a shock of red hair steps out. "I was trapped inside the house once," he says, his voice trembling slightly. "We couldn't even shatter the glass to get out. I only escaped when the house itself let me." He pauses for a moment, letting what he said sink in. "Doesn't it seem a little strange that not one of the windows in that place is broken after all these years?"

Everyone stares back at the mansion. It's true. The moonlight reflects off dozens of panes, but not one window is missing.

"Look, I'll show you," he adds. Gathering several rocks from the field, the red-haired man hurls them at the house. They hit several windows but bounce off harmlessly. "Now do you believe me?"

The crowd murmurs, and a number of people take a step back from the mansion. Sarah's mom shakes her head. "What are you all afraid of?" she asks the crowd. "The house was probably built with special, non-breakable glass. What's so spooky about—"

"You're wrong," interrupts an elderly woman. Old Mary Beth Hollingsworth, Amanda's grandma, steps to the forefront. "We shouldn't be so hasty to call anyone crazy. Many years ago, something horrible happened to me in that mansion, too," she says. "I found the body of my dear friend Anita Jardine in that terrible house!"

Everyone starts talking at once, relating a story about the mansion or responding to someone else's. Suddenly, Sarah feels a chill pass through her and she hugs her sweatshirt around her. At the same time she sees a faint green glow coming from the house's basement. She's about to say something, but it quickly disappears.

"The house is awakening," she murmurs.

But no one pays attention to her. For now, an earthly howling has begun. And the greenish glow has returned, only now it is enveloping the mansion completely.

Everybody gasps, and people begin tripping over each other as they scramble for the safety of the woods. Soon the whole town is huddling in the dark forest, watching as the mansion moans and spits out greenish rays of light.

"Let's burn the place down!" a man screams.

"Yeah, let's burn it to the ground!" another shouts.

Cigarette lighters and matches flicker as people break off branches and light them. Then a mob of angry people bearing flaming torches advances on the evil house.

Sarah and the other children have been told to stay back, and together they watch as the mansion expands. Sarah is sure it will rupture soon, unleashing the horrors that have been living within.

As flames lick up the mansion's sides, the adults rush back to the safety of the trees to be with their children. Suddenly a whooshing sound hisses from the mansion and it turns into a great mountain of fire. Burnt shutters fall to the ground. Gargoyles, their supporting rain gutters warped by the heat, fall from the roof like black cats leaping off fences. And finally, the stubborn windowpanes explode outward. Along with the crackling sound of the flames, a terrible moaning fills the night air, and then it slowly becomes a low, agonized scream, like the sound of something dying.

Standing in awe at the amazing sight, the crowd watches the Jardine mansion burn. And not until the entire house has become a smoking pile of rubble do the tired townspeople turn toward their homes.

Sarah's mother grips her hand, and forces out a smile as they turn and walk away. "It's over, honey," she says. "I'm sorry I didn't believe you."

But Sarah is not listening to her mother. All she can hear is the terrible laughter that is slowly rising up from behind them. Petrified of what she might see, Sarah slowly turns around and finds that her worst fear has been realized.

"No!" she screams. And then everyone turns around to gape in horror.

There, rising up once again in the barren meadow, is the house. Whole once more, it smokes slightly, but otherwise there is no sign that it has been touched by a single flame. Again the windows are intact, again the gargoyles perch on the roof.

The crowd screams, and suddenly they turn to find a new light glimmering brightly on the horizon. They run toward it, down the path and over the next hill. And there the townspeople stand, stunned and unbelieving. For except for the Jardine mansion, every house in town is on fire.